I0738544

# Also in the series:

Find these and other titles online at all major retailers, or contact us through www.ElizabethLeeSorrell.com to buy your own signed copy!

# THE CLAUSE Tradition

Elizabeth Lee Sorrell

trading as

Yarbrough House Publishing, Inc.

Trading as Yabrough House Publishing, Inc.
For information please email
info@yarbroughhousepublishing.com

www.YarbroughHousePublishing.com

ISBN 978-1-7330965-3-9

First Edition.

Printed in the United States of America

# Acknowledgements

I'd like to thank my family who really do all the hard work. While I sit back and make up fanciful stories, my family stays busy proofing, formatting, illustrating, crunching numbers, and taking care of all the "business stuff." All I do is play with my imagination, but my family works hard to bring life to my stories.

Chapter One

"I don't care about tradition, and I don't care what you say. I'm not doing it!" Noel screamed at her parents before stomping up the stairs and slamming her bedroom door.

"What happened to our sweet little girl?" Wynter sighed.

"She got replaced by a moody teenage monster," Anthony answered.

"She's always been like that," Shepard, pointed out about his sister, "but this time, I don't blame her. Can you even imagine Noel fighting a vampire? What is she going to do sic Roscoe on them?"

Roscoe was the family's very large, very domesticated pet polar bear.

"Roscoe can't go," Anthony reminded Shepard.

"Exactly, that's just one more point. Roscoe is getting old. Do you really think he would survive the separation? That bear thinks Noel is his."

"We'll talk about it later. Didn't you tell Papa and Gam that you would help them with repairs today?" Wynter asked.

"Yeah, I'm on my way."

Shepard walked out the door into the freezing cold. Wynter snuggled into Anthony's chest and sighed.

"What are we going to do with them?" she wondered.

"You were the one who wanted more than one," Anthony pointed out.

"Me? I don't remember you ever arguing."

"No, I wanted kids. They're good kids. Everything will work out."

"I hope you're right."

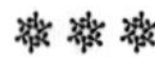

Tradition? Noel couldn't believe that her parents would even ask her to do that. Maybe she'd had enough tradition.

She knew her parents' story well. Dad had been a vampire and Mom saved him from himself. They fell in love despite the odds. She took a chance on a vampire, and they're still happily married today.

How could Noel be expected to hunt down and kill vampires? Kill others just like her dad? It felt like a betrayal to even entertain the idea. Mom and Dad didn't think so though. Her eighteenth birthday was one week away, and Clauses, excepting the oldest male, were expected to hunt and kill vampires after turning eighteen.

No one had pushed the training on Noel yet, but the closer her birthday came the more Mom and Dad wanted to talk about the future. Noel didn't know what the future held for her, but it certainly wasn't vampire hunting. She threw herself down on the bed with a huff. She would not cry. She would not.

Noel rolled her eyes with a cringe when someone knocked on the door. Mom didn't wait for an answer either. She pushed the door open and let herself inside. Noel rolled to the side, making room for Mom on the bed.

"It isn't fair," Noel said, beating her mom to the punch.

"I know, but, baby, life's not always fair. Did I ever tell you that Aunt Mary didn't want to do it either?"

"No, what happened?"

"Her father didn't give her a choice."

"Why does she do it?"

"I think that's something you should ask her for yourself," Mom said and laid the satellite phone next to Noel.

"She can't change my mind."

"It still wouldn't hurt to hear her take on it. Do you still want to go down to the South Pole for your birthday?" Mom asked.

"Yes." Of course she wanted to go to the South Pole. She loved it down there. Aunt Star was planning a big week for Noel's birthday. She had invited everyone to come stay for the week. She even rented out a whole hotel for the family.

Not that she'd be staying in the hotel. Angel, Gloria, and Noel were staying with Aunt Star and Uncle Declan in Angel's room. It was going to be great! Noel loved spending time with her family, especially when they could all be together, but Angel and Gloria were her two best friends in the whole world.

"That's good," Mom said. "Let's just enjoy the week, and we'll talk about the future later."

"Sure." Noel still wasn't going to hunt vampires, but there was no sense in telling Mom right now.

"Give Aunt Mary a call," Mom told Noel on her way out of the room. She shut the door behind her just like she found it, allowing Noel a sense of privacy.

Noel had a hard time figuring out her mom and Aunt Mary's relationship. Sometimes they seemed so close, and other times it was like Mom barely tolerated her. Dad said it was his fault that he had come between them back when Noel had still been a baby, but that couldn't be it. Could it? Dad and Aunt Mary were so close.

Noel didn't want to hear one more adult telling her what she had to do with the rest of her life; although, she was very curious why Aunt Mary hunted vampires if she had never wanted to do it in the first place.

"Hello?" Kris answered the phone. Kris Davis was Aunt Mary and Uncle Blaine's only child. Aunt Mary told Uncle Blaine that no way was she going through nine months of that again. Kris was five years younger than Noel, and Noel remembers Aunt Mary talking about how perfect her baby boy was and that she had to protect him. Uncle Blaine was not a vampire hunter, and truth be told, Noel thought it was more likely that Aunt Mary didn't want to be responsible for protecting more than the two men she already had to protect.

"Is Aunt Mary there?" Noel asked.

"Yeah. MOM," Kris hollered without moving the phone away from his mouth first.

"Hello?" Aunt Mary answered.

"Hey, Aunt Mary."

"Noel, what a surprise. Are you getting excited about your birthday coming up?"

"I'm more excited about spending a week in the South Pole."

Aunt Mary chuckled. "Eighteen years ago, I never would have dreamed those words would ever come out of a Clause's mouth."

"Yeah." There was some stupid feud between the North Pole and South Pole up until Noel was a preschooler, so she really didn't remember it. "Mom said you didn't want to be a vampire hunter when you were my age. Is that true?"

"Oh, that's what this is about. No, at your age the last thing I wanted was to be a vampire hunter. It was the most horrible thing I could imagine ever doing. I didn't want to fight. I didn't want to kill, and I didn't want to ever be that close to monsters."

"Aunt Mary, Dad was a vampire!" Noel gasped unbelieving.

"He sure was, and I wanted him dead so badly it blinded me to a lot. I tried so many times to kill him."

"Aunt Mary! I thought you and Dad are friends."

"We are now, but we weren't always. Even after he married your mom, I didn't want to believe that he had changed, that he wasn't the monster I knew him to be."

"What happened?"

"Well, your dad happened. Even though I hated him, he was there for me when I needed him. If it hadn't been for your dad, I wouldn't have ever married your Uncle Blaine. He wouldn't let me give up on love, and together we sort of saved each other."

"Dad needed saving?" Noel asked incredulously.

"Oh yeah, your dad knew the monster he had been as much as I did."

"My dad's not a monster!"

"No, he's not. Your dad is a good man."

"He is… So, why do you do it?"

"Why do I hunt vampires?"

"Yeah."

"I have seen up close and personal just what vampires are capable of doing. I didn't want the job all those years ago, but I can see now why my dad insisted."

"Why?"

"It is an important job. It's my job to protect people who are not capable of protecting themselves. You've made the Christmas Eve run with your dad before. You've probably seen his naughty and nice list before. All those kids are vulnerable. Their parents are just as helpless as the children. They'll never know who protects them. They'll never know the threat against them, because of us, Clauses who are willing to fight to protect others."

"You make it sound like it's some great calling."

"It is."

"That's great and all, but I just don't know that it is my calling… Aunt Star doesn't do it."

"She did."

"What? Aunt Star?"

"Yeah, it's hard to picture her some great warrior, isn't it?"

"Definitely hard."

"Aunt Star quit to marry Declan and move to the South Pole to be with him, but she spent centuries fighting. She was good too. She was so good. In fact, she was the only person I've ever known who could fight vampires in high heels."

"No way!" Noel laughed.

"Yes way, have you ever seen Aunt Star wear anything besides high heels?"

Noel thought about it for a minute. "No, even her slippers are high heels, the kind with the poufy feathers."

"Yeah, she was an amazing huntress. So, why all the questions?"

"I told Mom and Dad that I wasn't going to hunt vampires. It just isn't right. My dad was a vampire."

"Have you talked to your parents about that?" Aunt Mary asked.

"I told them I wouldn't do it."

"I get that, but did you tell them why you felt that way?"

"Not exactly."

"Hmm, Noel, if you're thinking about showing mercy to vampires, don't. Your dad would be the first to tell you, it isn't safe. Your dad was never a typical vampire. There has never been another like your dad, and there never will be. Talk to him, sweetheart."

"Sure."

"Promise me."

"Mom said to enjoy our week in the South Pole, and we'll talk about it when we get back."

"Good, make sure you tell them everything you're feeling and why you are feeling that way."

"I will. Thanks, Aunt Mary."

"Love you, Noel. We'll see you next week."

Well, that hadn't been a real answer. Noel was no closer to understanding Aunt Mary than she was her parents.

# Chapter Two

Noel, Angel, and Gloria laughed as they did each other's nails. They were sitting in Angel's room, which was amazing! Aunt Star believed in letting Angel, Joy, and Nickolas decorate their own rooms. Aunt Star's only rule was that they keep the doors shut so that in her words, "all the magical chaos won't seep out into my finely decorated house." Angel's style was so much like her mother's, it wouldn't have mattered anyway. As long as it was glittery and pretty, it was a keeper.

Right now, though, the girls were getting ready to go out to the ice rink with Angel's dad. Uncle Declan had a couple of one on one hockey sessions today, but he had promised the girls they could have half the ice on the condition that they stayed out of the way and did not cause a distraction for his students.

"Dad said hurry up. He's leaving in two minutes," Nickolas said poking his head in the door.

"Knock first," Angel said slinging the door shut with a flick of her finger.

Nickolas reopened the door and added, "Dad also said last week that if you don't quit slamming doors, he was going to take your door off the hinges. Then Mom would decorate your room for you."

"Shut up," Angel told her annoying little brother.

"I don't know why you girls are painting your nails just to go to the skate rink anyway."

"It's a girl thing, Nicky," Aunt Star said walking up behind Nickolas and kissing him on the top of his head. "You girls about ready?"

"Coming," Gloria said, popping off the bed.

"Mom, you know I hate it when you call me Nicky."

"That's what I named you," Aunt Star pouted.

"You named me Nickolas. Call me that or Nick even. Just don't call me Nicky."

With a long-suffering sigh, Aunt Star said, "My baby isn't a baby anymore. Maybe it's time I talked with Declan about having another baby."

"NO!" Angel and Nickolas shouted in unison.

Noel thought the whole thing was hilarious, because if Aunt Star wanted another baby, she'd get one. Uncle Declan would give her anything she wants.

"Quit yelling at your mother," Uncle Declan scolded from the bottom of the stairs. "Girls lets go."

The girls had their skates laced up and were on the ice before Uncle Declan's first student got there. They claimed their half of the rink and took off in loops and twirls.

"Noah's nephew is coming today," Angel said.

"Noah? Mom's friend?" Noel asked.

"He's the one."

"I thought Noah didn't have any kids."

"He doesn't. Lorelei can't have kids," Gloria told.

Noel and Angel looked at Gloria like she had grown a second head. With a negligent shrug Gloria added, "Uncle North still stays in touch with Lorelei."

"It's actually kind of sad. She would have made a great mother," Angel added.

"So, what do we care if Noah's nephew is going to be here?" Noel wondered. "Noah's brother doesn't even like our family."

"Noah is one of Dad's best friends. I heard Noah telling Dad and Kyson one time that he thinks Ethan made a mistake. Apparently, your mom and Ethan were good friends once upon a time. Anyway, Noah thinks he misses your mom but is too stubborn to apologize and let it go. Ethan isn't the point though. It's his son, Kellen, that I'm talking about, and Kellen is hot."

Gloria tried to act like she didn't care, but Noel could tell she was interested. Noel didn't care how good this guy looked. His family couldn't stand the Clauses, and that sort of thing never changes.

"Who cares how he looks? His family hates the Clause family, and don't think for a minute that just because you two have a different last name that they've forgotten for a minute that deep down you're still Clauses. You're wasting your time with a guy like him," Noel lectured.

"I didn't say I wanted to date him, Noel," Angel snapped. "He's way to full of himself to make good boyfriend material. That doesn't mean he isn't fun to look at."

"Don't let Aunt Mary hear you say that," Gloria laughed.

Any talk about boys equaled dependence on boys in Aunt Mary's book. Aunt Mary was very much in love with Uncle Blaine, but she still lectured the girls all the time about the importance of standing on their own two feet. Kris had no idea how lucky he was to be a boy. Uncle Blaine used to joke and say that was why they stopped having kids after Kris. Used to, because the last time he said it, Aunt Mary caught him.

Noel looked up as a young boy, no older than ten, skated out onto the ice with Uncle Declan. "I hope that's not the guy you were talking about?" Noel laughed.

Noel laughed even harder when Gloria joined in the laughter.

"Of course not!" Angel said indignantly. "Kellen is a senior. That makes him older than me and Gloria. He's dad's second appointment today."

Gloria was two and a half years younger than Noel, and Angel was three and a half years younger. The age gap had never mattered much to the girls. They had been really close for as long as Noel could remember.

It was an indoor rink, so it didn't take the girls long to get warmed up. They shed their extra layers and left them to the side before lining up to race, not that Noel or Gloria stood a chance against Angel. Angel was fast, wicked fast. Uncle Declan said that she would be an asset for the hockey team, but Angel wasn't interested. Instead, Aunt Star got her signed up for figure skating lessons from a very young age. Angel taught Noel and Gloria everything she learned just because the girls always shared everything.

Right now, though, it was all about speed as the three girls lined up on one side. As soon as Gloria called, "Go!" all three girls took off. Wind was blowing through Noel's hair. Angel was in the lead, of course, but that wasn't the point. Noel could get a little too competitive at times; however, the girls weren't overly competitive with each other. They just liked skating fast. It was an adrenaline rush, and even though Angel was the fastest, Noel and Gloria weren't slow. The girls could probably out skate most of Uncle Declan's students.

Blood was pumping as the world flew past Noel in a blur. They were just skating back and forth as fast as they could now. All semblance of a race was gone. Noel couldn't wipe the stupid grin off her face. The only thing better than this kind of speed was playing with Roscoe.

Speaking of which, Roscoe was stuck at home with the elves this week. She sure hoped the elves didn't forget to feed him. Dad assured Noel that Roscoe would be fine. It wasn't fair that they had to leave him behind. He was from the South Pole after all, but Mom said that he was getting too old and too domesticated to make the trip. It still wasn't right. Roscoe would have loved having other polar bears to play with.

Noel was so lost in thought, she crashed right into Angel who had planted herself in Noel's path. Angel then reached out to grab Gloria's arm as she went past, stopping her too.

"What are you doing?" Gloria demanded.

"That is Kellen Nickola," Angel announced in a conspiratorial whisper.

Noel looked over to where Uncle Declan was talking to a new arrival.

"Wow," Gloria breathed.

"Doesn't look much like Noah, does he?" Noel said dismissively.

"Who cares," Gloria said practically drooling. Traitor. This guy hated them just because of who their parents were. How could Gloria and Angel take his side?

"He has blue eyes like Noah," Angel corrected, "except his are way deeper."

"Deeper?" Noel questioned.

"Yeah deep like the ocean."

"Whatever." Noel couldn't see his eyes from this far across the ice, but nothing else looked like Noah. Noah had dark brown hair, but this guy's hair was much darker, almost black. It wasn't as dark as Noel's jet black curls but close. He was tan too. What normal person from the South Pole has a tan? He wasn't built like Noah either. Noah was lean muscles; this guy had packed on muscles. He must have worked out, a lot. This guy wasn't even smiling. Noah was almost always smiling. It was what made him so pleasant to be around. This Kellen guy looked like he was concentrating, like he was hanging on every word Uncle Declan said.

That was another thing he didn't have in common with Noah. Noah was more interested in animals. He didn't have time for hockey. Liking hockey wasn't a bad thing though. Uncle Declan liked hockey. He'd even made it his career. That didn't make Kellen great though, neither did the fact that he looked good. Not that Noel was going to admit he looked good.

"Are we going to skate or what?" Noel asked.

"You go ahead," Gloria waved.

"What did we come here for if we aren't going to skate?" Noel protested.

"We came here for that," Angel said indicating the other end of the rink where Uncle Declan had Kellen doing drills. Angel and Gloria were practically drooling. It was embarrassing.

"Not me. I came to skate," Noel said and took off.

Gloria and Angel pretended to skate, just not successfully. It was blatantly obvious that they were watching Kellen. For her part, Noel was ignoring Kellen and both the other girls. She had come here to have fun, and that was what she was going to do even if she had to do it alone.

They had been there a while, and Kellen's time had to be almost up when Uncle Declan called out, "Girls, think y'all could give us a hand?"

Noel followed a far too eager Angel and Gloria to where Uncle Declan waited with Kellen.

"What's up," Angel croaked. Gloria giggled, and Noel rolled her eyes.

"Suit up," Uncle Declan said pointed to some extra padding equipment. "Kellen is going to take some shots at the goal, and I want you girls to add some resistance."

"Three against one?" Noel questioned.

"Sure, that way if he makes a goal. He'll know he earned it."

Noel knew the basic theory of hockey, but she had never actually played before. She and Shepard were the only kids at the North Pole, and two people didn't make a hockey team. Still, a challenge was a challenge. Noel was not one to back down from a challenge, and Uncle Declan knew that.

The girls strapped the padding around themselves and lined up in front of the goal. Angel was right about one thing. This guy was definitely full of himself. He leered at the girls with a cocky grin.

A slap to the back of the head from Uncle Declan wiped the grin from his face. "That's my daughter and nieces, delinquent. The point of this exercise is to get you to think about your game not think about girls."

Kellen shrugged then put his game face on. Concentration radiated off him like a physical wave. If that wasn't a challenge, Noel didn't know what was.

Kellen lined up the puck and took his first shot. Gloria and Angel both squealed and dove in different directions. Noel dove at the puck and stopped it. Ouch! That hurt, but she wasn't going to let on that the arrogant male in front of her had hurt her.

"Good stop," Uncle Declan praised. Then he shook his head in the direction of his daughter sprawled out on the ice to his far right. "Angel what are you and Gloria doing?"

"It's called self-preservation, Dad. Let Noel do it."

Way to sell your cousin out, Noel thought.

"Again," Uncle Declan told Kellen.

Kellen did, shot after shot. He took so many shots that Noel lost count. Best of all, he only got one past her. He wouldn't have gotten that one if Angel hadn't been cheering the previous stop and raining glitter down on the ice. What was surprising was that Uncle Declan didn't say anything about the glitter. All those years with Aunt Star must have desensitized Uncle Declan to all the glitzy girliness.

"I think that's enough for today," Uncle Declan finally said. "Noel, you're a natural! We've got to talk your parents into getting you signed up for hockey."

"Yeah right, who would I play with? Shepherd?"

"Nah, we'd sign you up for one of the teams down here. You could stay with us during hockey season."

"I'll let you run that idea by Mom and Dad," Noel teased.

"Good point," Uncle Declan laughed.

Noel started to skate off to put the pads up but was stopped by Gloria and Angel. Gloria elbowed Noel, and Angel gave a pointed look in Kellen's direction.

A look back at Kellen showed him staring at the girls' retreating backs while Uncle Declan retrieved hockey pucks.

"What's he looking at?"

"You!" Angel delighted.

Great, he was probably contemplating ways to kill the daughter of Santa.

Chapter Three

Meals were always a big production when the Clauses got together. Since everyone had gathered in the South Pole this time, Aunt Star felt responsible for cooking. Big mistake. Anyone who had ever seen Aunt Star cook before knew it would be a disaster, but they let her try anyway. It ended with Mom clearing out a house full of smoke.

Dad and Papa thought it was hilarious. They just laughed and laughed. On Papa, it looked jolly. His belly shook and shook with laughter. Dad, not so much. Dad laughed just as hard as Papa, but he had no belly to shake, which was just wrong for Santa. Nothing for it though. Dad ate more than anyone Noel knew, but the man was still rail thin.

Aunt Mary and her best friend Vivienne started talking about take out after the cooking fiasco. They weren't very cooks either. If it had been left up to Aunt Star, Aunt Mary, and Vivienne, they probably would have ordered take out. They almost did too, but Noel knew Gam wouldn't let it go that far.

Before any orders could be placed Gam and Mom were in the kitchen along with Aunt Marci, Uncle North's wife. It wasn't long before both Uncle Israel's daughters, Faith and Bell, joined in. Faith was Gloria's mom, who had only just gotten to the South Pole. Most of the Clauses had Christmas related names. Christmas was the family business after all. Well, that and vampire hunting, but that was something Noel wasn't ready to think about. How would one even go about naming a child after the vocation of vampire hunting? Noel smiled to herself as she thought about it. Let's see; there was the ever-popular Buffy, Hunter, or Chase.

Their family linage could get pretty confusing for people on the outside looking in. It started out because Papa had so many brothers and sisters. He had three brothers and two sisters. Yep, six of them all together; his parents must have felt like they were living in a zoo, especially with the hustle and bustle of the Santa job. Aunt Star and Aunt Mary got married so late in life that their kids were the same age as Papa and Uncle Israel's grandkids. Uncle North's grandkids even were gown. That was because he had been the first to get married. He had four kids, Peace, Carol, Frost, and Hope. Peace had one son, Nick. Carol had two boys, Yule and Garland. Frost had a boy and two girls, Christian, Holly, and Kristen. Hope had two kids, Ivy and North, named after his grandfather. Things could always get crazier yet. Uncle Joseph still wasn't married. He was a fun, good looking guy. Noel didn't know what he was waiting on.

Plus, Kyson and Vivienne were there with their three boys, Calder, Harding, and Trumble. Vivienne and Kyson both loved hockey, and Noel sometimes wondered if Vivienne was trying to have her own hockey team. All three boys loved hockey as much as their parents.

Technically Kyson and Vivienne and their kids weren't family. They weren't blood related at least. Kyson was one of Uncle Declan's best friends, Noah being the other, and Vivienne was Aunt Mary's best friend. They were around for so many family functions that they might as well have been family.

Everyone was there so far except for Uncle Joseph, Uncle Israel and his wife Aunt Heidi. Uncle Israel and Aunt Heidi would be here in a couple days. Who knew when Uncle Joseph would show up. Still, that was a lot of people to put under one roof to eat together. It was loud, and there were always multiple conversations going on at one time. That was why Aunt Star let the ten kids set up a table in the basement to eat. The basement was normally used as a playroom, but for mealtimes this week it was the kids dining area. Uncle Declan and Kyson said it was because the kids were too loud, but Noel was pretty sure it was more so that the adults could have their own conversations without having to watch what they said in front of the kids.

"Hold up, you three," Aunt Mary said stopping Noel, Gloria, and Angel on their way to the basement. "You three are the oldest. You're in charge. Keep an eye on the others."

"Yes, ma'am," the girls answered in chorus.

Nickolas, Aunt Star's nine-year-old, came to the table in one of his dad's old hockey jerseys. "I'm going to go play hockey tomorrow. Dad said so. He said tomorrow is boy day."

"That's not fair!" Joy protested. She was twelve. "I didn't get to go today."

"You're not a boy," Nickolas felt propelled to point out.

Noel felt kind of bad for Joy. Now that she thought about it, Joy was the only girl who didn't go today. She was only two and a half years younger than Angel, but it felt like such a gap.

"That's all right," Shepherd stepped in. "You can go with us. You can be on my team."

"I call Calder," Kris said.

"Fine, but I'm on Shepherd and Joy's team," Nickolas pouted. Funny how Nickolas wanted to play with his sister all of a sudden now that Shepherd was playing with her.

"I'm with Nicolas," said Trumble, also nine years old.

"Guess you're with me and Calder," Kris told Harding. Those three were like doorsteps. Calder was twelve. Kris was eleven, and Harding was ten. From the look the three shared, Noel got the impression they played together a lot. It wasn't surprising since Kris's mom, Aunt Mary, and Calder, Harding, and Trumble's mom, Vivienne, were best friends.

"I bet the other three girls didn't even play hockey today," Shepherd commented.

"Actually, we did. Thank you very much," Angel smarted back.

"Well, sort of," Gloria corrected timidly.

"Sort of? What does that mean?" Kris asked.

"Dad had Kellen taking shots at the goal. He wanted us to block the shot. Gloria and I sort of bailed, but Noel only let one get past her," Angel described.

"Declan let you play with Kellen Nickola?" Calder asked Noel. "Is he trying to lose his job?"

"How would that cause him to lose his job?" Noel demanded. That was an insulting comment. Granted, she didn't know that much about hockey, but she wasn't totally useless.

"Kellen Nickola is Ethan Nickola's son."

"So?"

"No offence, but Ethan Nickola hates your mom."

"Well, that's too bad. He'll just have to get over it."

"I'm sure Uncle Declan knows what he's doing," Shepherd assured them all. "So, you were pretty good, huh?"

"Uncle Declan said I was a natural," Noel bragged.

"Maybe we could get a family game up while we're here this week," Gloria suggested.

"You can't run from the puck," Noel grinned.

"Maybe we can do something else instead," Gloria back tracked.

"You should have seen Noel today," Angel told Shepherd. "She was really good, tough too."

"Yeah," Gloria agreed. "I don't know why she doesn't want to hunt vampires. She's one of the toughest people I know."

"Wait. What?" Calder interrupted. "You don't want to be a vampire hunter? That would be such a cool job! I'm thinking about asking Mary to train me."

"Why not my mom?" Joy wanted to know.

"Your mom does everything with glitter."

"So?"

Nickolas scoffed, "Don't be dumb. Boys don't fight with glitter."

"Whatever, I don't fight at all," Noel said putting the subject to rest.

"Are you going to hunt vampires?" Trumble asked Shepherd.

"Can't."

"Why not?"

"I'm the oldest male. I'll be taking over the job of Santa for Dad someday."

"Yeah, Dad loves being Santa. It could be years. All you're expected to do is laze around until Dad gets too old to keep going," Noel accused.

"Hey, it's not my fault. You're just mad because you don't want your future decided for you," Shepherd shot back.

"You do?" Angel reacted.

"It's just the way things are done in our family," Gloria spoke up. "Granddaddy is a vampire hunter. Mom is a vampire hunter, and I'll be a vampire hunter one day. That's just how it works. Your mom was a vampire hunter until she retired to marry your dad and move down here. You'll be a vampire hunter one day too."

"No, I won't," Angel retorted.

"You don't have a choice in the matter. Hey, maybe we can all three work together!"

"Nice try, Gloria, but I already told you, I'm not going to do it. No one's going to make me either. I'm no one's slave," Noel declared.

"Why don't you two swap places?" Calder asked pointing between Noel and Shepherd.

"Yeah right, a female Santa? What if I ever got caught? The whole world would freak out over a girl Santa."

"The world would freak out either way. The humans don't want to know there are vampires running around killing and drinking blood. My mom told me so, told me not to tell people about vampires," Kris told them all.

"He has a point," Joy agreed.

"Why are we even having this conversation?" Noel challenged.

"Gloria started it," Harding reminded them.

"Fine, I'm ending it."

"Fine by me," Joy said. "Guess what I heard Mom talking about today. A dance! She said that Aunt Mary and Anthony both love to dance. She said it would be great to plan a dance while they were down here."

"Awesome," Gloria said.

Kris groaned, "Mom and Dad get mushy when they dance together."

"I'll dance with you, and we'll dance like men," Shepherd offered.

"Me to," Nickolas inserted.

"That's right. We'll get a big group together, no girls allowed."

For all his annoying traits, Shepherd really was a pretty good peace maker.

## Chapter Four

The next morning everyone ate breakfast in shifts. It wasn't to make enough room for everybody or anything, even though that would have been a good idea. It was because everyone got up at different times. Mom did that at home a lot too. Gam was never that laxed at home though. Gam's rule was if you weren't up when breakfast was served, you just didn't eat, and that was why Noel hardly ever slept over at Papa and Gam's anymore.

Noel, Gloria, and Angel were the last three to eat. Aunt Marci was quiet, shy, but boy, could she cook!

"I think I'm in love with your pancakes, Aunt Marci," Noel complimented around a big bite of pancake.

"Yeah, think you could teach me to make these?" Angel asked. Then with a somber tone, she added, "Mom is a lost cause."

That got a laugh out of even Aunt Marci.

"I heard that, young lady," Aunt Star said as she walked into the kitchen. "It's true. You'll have to choose though, new dress or pancakes."

"I choose pancakes," Angel said without deliberation. "I have plenty of dresses."

"Looks like it just us then," Aunt Star said to Noel and Gloria.

"What?" Gloria asked for clarification.

"We're going to have a dance, and you two are going to need dresses."

That got Noel and Gloria eating faster.

After breakfast Aunt Marci started showing Angel the finer points of cooking while Aunt Star took Noel and Gloria to her shop.

Aunt Star had started her own line of clothing after moving to the South Pole, and the shop was amazing. Aunt Star had the most beautiful clothes.

"Oh, Aunt Star, it's all so beautiful," Gloria marveled.

"They really are good," Noel agreed as she ran her hand along a short pink dress with an empire waist and sequined bodice. "You do such good work. Are the others coming to choose a dress too?"

"Actually... It's just us girls. Everyone else left it up to my judgement. You know what that means? You get first choice, and the others will all get whatever we give them."

Noel and Gloria walked around eyeing the dresses. There was so much to choose from.

"What are you wearing?" Gloria asked Aunt Star.

"Sparkle, naturally." Aunt Star held up a long-sleeved dress that would fall mid-calf. It was form-fitting and every inch covered in red sequins. "I'm still debating between silver glittered heels or green glittered shoes."

"Silver would look amazing," Gloria said.

"Yeah, but green and red are a Clause's best colors," Noel teased.

"Right?" Aunt Star continued ignoring the sarcasm. "I've got dresses galore that are Christmas themed. I know it's not Christmas time, but it might be nice if we all dressed up with a Christmas look."

"Oh? You're serious?" Gloria asked.

"Well, sure."

"Maybe," Noel offered vaguely and continued to peruse the dresses.

"Girls look at this and tell me what you think." Aunt Star held up a long straight evening gown with spaghetti straps. It was a classic, simple design done in silver sequins. "I was thinking about this for Mary. That girl could use a night of glamor."

"I love it," Noel answered and turned to Gloria.

"I think Aunt Mary will love it," Gloria added.

"Excellent! Silver sequins it is!" Aunt Star thrilled. She really did love dressing people up in pretty clothes.

"What about the guys?" Noel wondered.

"Tuxes of course. I'll put some in red vests and some in green, but they'll all have holly boutonnieres.

"So, all the guys are going with a Christmas theme?" Gloria noted.

"That's the price they pay for showing such little interest in their outfits," Aunt Star tisked.

"Haaa!" Gloria gasped suddenly. "Aunt Star, what about this one?" she asked clutching a satin green, full length ball gown. It was strapless, gathered into a knot just under the bust line, and flared out at the hips.

"You like it?" Aunt Star smiled. "Try it on, and let's get it fitted."

"Really, I can wear this one?"

"Wear it? Honey, you can keep it. It's a gift from me to you."

"Oh, Aunt Star, I love you! I love you! I love you!"

Noel continued looking about while Aunt Star and Gloria got just the right fit. Soon she came to a deep red, long sleeved dress. The wrists were fur lined and boasting an extra ruffle extension. The bodice had a gold embroidered pattern. The same pattern spread out to adorn the full skirt. A fur lined overlay finished off the dress that was clearly meant for Mrs. Clause. It was elegant and absolutely perfect for Gam.

Hanging nearby was a green velvet dress with three quarter length sleeves and a full skirt. The V-neck was lined with fur as well as the sleeves, skirt, and appropriate hood. It was accessorized by a wide black belt. It was Mrs. Clause the second edition personified. It fit Mom to a tee. It was Mrs. Clause, but still just Mama.

Noel held up the two dresses. "Aunt Star, how about these for Mom and Gam?"

Aunt Star gave Noel an adoring smile and nodded. "I think that is just about right, but what about you, Noel. Have you found a dress for yourself yet?"

"Not yet. I'll keep looking."

Gloria and Aunt Star were circling throughout the dresses again when Noel and Gloria stopped in front of a white muslin dress. It had short puff sleeves. A holly pattern wrapped around the empire waist line just like the sleeves and bottom of the dress. It was heavenly and all Christmas. The girls looked at each other and together they said, "Angel."

They showed it to Aunt Star who said, "That was the exact dress I had in mind for her."

Next Noel eyed a velvet, halter dress. It was a dark red, and the skirt was so full it looked like a Christmas dress fit for *Gone With the Wind*. White flowers vined across the top of the bodice and above a ring of ruffles that hung roughly six inches from the bottom. It was so beautiful and had its own Mrs. Clause quality to it. Noel loved the dress, but she wouldn't feel right dressing the part of Mrs. Clause.

"Can Grandma wear this one?" Gloria asked holing up a full length strapless dress. The top was a very plain black. The bottom, however, was made of a very flowing, gauzy material. The waistline started black and faded into reds and greens which then faded out to white at the bottom.

"Heidi will look lovely in that," Aunt Star sighed happily.

"That is gorgeous," Noel agreed.

"Look, how playful this one is," Gloria said holding up a red flapper dress. The straps were wide strips of white which also trimmed the bottom of the dress. There were long, red gloves that were trimmed with the same wide white. It even had a red head band with mistletoe.

Noel laughed at the whimsical nature of the dress. "That one has Bell's name written all over it."

"You think?" Aunt Star questioned.

"Oh yes! It's perfect for Aunt Bell!" Gloria joined in.

"Well, if you girls say so," Aunt Star conceded. "I want to find something special for Marci. She's just so shy, I want to find something that stands out and will show off her natural beauty."

Noel held up a short, one shouldered, green dress. It was slightly full without looking childish, and a narrow black belt completed it. "What about this one? Aunt Marci has great legs."

"Aunt Marci does have great legs," Gloria nodded solemnly.

"She does, doesn't she, but what about those curves. She's so curvy. That's what I remember most about Marci from when I was growing up. I wanted to have curves just like Marci when I grew up."

"Mission accomplished," Gloria said, causing both girls to fall into peals of laughter.

"Yes, well, curves are an asset. Let's see if we can find one to show off her amazing curves," Aunt Star instructed.

"This one's nice," Noel choked out through her giggling. She held her hand up to point toward a red off the shoulder dress. It nipped in at the waist and was made to fit like a glove until it flared midway down the thighs.

"Oh, that's it!" Aunt Star said jumping up and down like a little girl.

That made Noel and Gloria fall out laughing all over again. Aunt Star was so much fun!

"That dress will show off her curves and her butt. Have either of you seen Marci in a pencil skirt?"

Noel and Gloria looked at each other and shook their heads.

"I can't believe I forgot about her butt!"

This time the girls just sat down in the floor laughing at Aunt Star.

"She has a butt to put all other Clause women to shame. Any dress that didn't show off that bum of hers just wouldn't do her justice. That dress will do the job quite nicely. Alright, off the floor girls. We still have more dresses to find. Noel have you found yours yet?"

"No ma'am, not yet."

"Then I suggest you get looking." Aunt Star held up a red dress that was strapless. It was fur trimmed on the top and bottom and had a big white bow at the waist. "Do you think my Joy can still wear this, or is it too little girlish?"

It was borderline childish with that big bow, but it was also strapless. Noel remembered how grown up she had felt when she got her first strapless dress. Aunt Star had given it to her, and she cherished that dress. "I think it will work fine."

"It's a little grown up and a little kid like too, just like Joy," Gloria concurred.

Aunt Star gave a both sad and put-upon sigh. "Sometimes I think both my girls are going on thirty. Where did the time go?"

Gloria pushed to her feet and moved to a green dress. It was sleeveless. It was high necked, and it had lace overlaying the waist. "It's modest. It's simple. It's Mom," Gloria stated directly.

"You know your mother's style well," Aunt Star complimented.

"Yeah, well, she's tried for years to make me dress more like her."

"You can thank Israel for that. He over protected both his girls. He insisted they dress extremely

conservatively. It was pounded into their heads until they didn't know any other way."

Gloria shrugged and walked away. That was old news.

Noel moved on until her eyes landed on ivy snaked around the waist of a white dress. It climbed up and slithered down from the waist. It was a short, strapless dress with a fun, fringed skirt.

"What do you think?" Aunt Star asked softly from behind.

"Ivy?"

"Very good choice," Aunt Star congratulated and kissed the temple of Noel's head. "The white dress would contrast with Ivy's dark skin nicely."

Noel wondered sometimes if these shopping trips were Aunt Star's way of passing on her trade and love of clothes.

Before long, Noel was back to the red velvet dress she had admired earlier. It was a timeless dress. Noel could see herself waltzing with her dad and his old-world charm that showed itself when he danced. Oh, how she longed to dress up like a classic Clause and dance the night away, but she was no classic Clause.

She was the granddaughter of the former Santa and daughter of the current Santa, yet the classic North Pole life was lost to her. Everyone wanted her to take up vampire hunting like countless Clauses before. Her eyes began to mist up, and Noel moved on quickly before she had time to cry.

Noel fingered a crimson dress of velvet. It wasn't overly fancy. It was a straight, floor length dress that was gathered around the bust.

"That looks like something Carol would like," Gloria said. "Want me to go run it past Aunt Star?"

"Sure."

The timeless red dress was still calling to Noel. She walked past it again. She just wanted to see it again. Finally, she stopped beside a rack with two similar dresses. Both were bright, Christmas red. Both were mermaid style fitting tight until right about the knee. One had a layer of tulle overlaying the flare at the bottom, and one had folds in the front that fit together beneath rhinestone snowflakes.

Holly had very similar tastes as Hope, her aunt. It was fitting that they wear such similar dresses.

"Aunt Star?" Noel called.

"Oh, I love those two. They were so much fun, and they turned out just lovely," Aunt Star described.

"What do you think about Hope and Holly?"

Aunt Star gave the dresses a contemplative look and said, "I think that just might work. That only leaves you and Kristen. What are you waiting on, precious?"

"I'm still looking," Noel shrugged. "I want to find just the right dress."

"I wouldn't expect anything less from you," Aunt Star said, and she pushed an errant curl out of Noel's face. Aunt Star had a soft spot for Noel. Aunt Mary had been Mom's favorite aunt growing up, but Noel shared a special bond with Aunt Star.

"Come look at this!" Gloria called out excitedly.

The dress Gloria had found was red and white. Strapless, it was gathered vertically across the bust. Underneath the bust lay a ring of lace featuring a vine of white flowers all the way around. The material gathered horizontally beneath the ring of lace. White flowers began over the left hip and flowed downward to circle around the thighs. From there the red wrapped asymmetrically over the white skirt. Lace was embroidered on the white here and there as well as to the hem of the skirt.

"It's so beautiful. Surely someone can wear it," Gloria was practically pleading.

"Kristen?" Aunt Star suggested, knowing that Spirit and Noel were the only two left.

"Yes!" Gloria was overjoyed.

"Good, now why don't you help Noel find a dress?"

Noel and Gloria split up once more in search for the dress that would work for Noel. This time Aunt Star trailed behind Noel. After a few minutes, Noel approached a black dress. It was a strapless dress that flared full at the waist. Poinsettias were attached across the bust line and flowed down the right side of the dress. It was dark to be sure, but poinsettias were the Christmas flower, right?

"Noel? Please tell me you aren't seriously considering that dress," Aunt Star intruded on Noel's thoughts. "You have all those midnight curls. You need a dress that will play towards your beautiful locks, not down play them."

"Noel! Hurry, you have to see this!" Gloria was screaming like the place was on fire.

Noel and Aunt Star rushed to where Gloria was waiting in front of the dress Noel had been eyeing all day.

"It's beautiful, isn't it?" Noel said wistfully.

"It's you!" Gloria insisted.

"I think we found a winner," Aunt Star agreed.

"I couldn't," Noel argued.

"Why not?" they both challenged.

"It's too... too Mrs. Clause."

"I don't think it's too Mrs. Clause at all," Aunt Star disputed. "I think it is too Miss Clause, and for that, my dear, you fit the bill."

"You really think so?"

"I do."

"Me too!" Gloria jumped up and down.

"Well... ok."

It took Aunt Star just a minute to alter it to fit Noel perfectly. Noel had the perfect Christmas dress to wear to a party in mid-January.

## Chapter Five

The next morning when Noel woke up, Uncle Israel and Heidi were there. The whole family was together now except for Uncle Joseph. What could be keeping him? The only one of Papa's brothers and sisters still unwed. Did that have something to do with it?

Married to his work, probably. All the more reason Noel wanted to have nothing to do with the trade. She didn't want killing to become her entire life, her entire reason for living. It was such a hypocritical thing to do, to kill others like her own dad. If that wasn't enough the killing would consume her until it became her entire being. She was too much like her dad. She had too much joy and happiness overflowing to acclimate to a life of violence and death. She didn't have it in her.

But, that wasn't what this trip was about, so she pushed the thoughts away and joined in the merriment of family togetherness. The boys talked incessantly about their hockey game the day before. Noel was glad to hear that even Joy had enjoyed it.

The women all went in turn to let Aunt Star make alterations to the dresses that the girls had chosen for each one. After Joy's alterations, she paraded around the house for everyone to see her new dress.

"Look, Bubba, I look like you now. Ho, ho, ho," Joy smiled proudly at her pitiful impersonation. All Papa's brothers and sisters had gone back to calling him Bubba like they had before their dad Santa Sr. passed away. Papa was technically Santa Jr., but he'd always be Papa to her.

Dad did the job of Santa now, but everyone still called him Anthony. Dad still calls Papa Santa. He says that Papa will always be Santa to him. The family laughs at that, but Mom and Noel got it. It was their thing, their bond. Dad looks up to Papa, and Mom says that everyone needs someone to look up to. Noel had asked Mom once who she looked up to. Mom said she looked up to Gam. Noel, who was young at the time, thought it must have been a parent thing, so Noel naturally looked up to her Mom. It didn't change anything though. Mom was still wrong about this vampire hunting thing.

"Oh, now, I don't know about that," Papa said pulling Joy into his lap. Joy looked up at Papa with wounded eyes, so Papa continued. "I think you look more and more like your mother every day, and she is a mighty pretty lady to take after."

"I do look like Mama," Joy agreed with a smile. Actually, Joy did look an awful lot like Aunt Star. Uncle Declan was going to have his hands full when Joy got older and the boys began to notice.

"Run take your dress off so you don't get it dirty before the dance," Aunt Star told Joy.

"Can't I wear it just a few more minutes?"

"Joy Anderson," Uncle Declan said in a calm voice. He didn't even raise his voice, and Joy took off running like her feet were on fire. That made everyone laugh.

Noel didn't really understand Joy's drive to obey her dad quicker than her mom. Oh, Noel understood the power of a dad, because her dad had always had that effect on her too. Aunt Star, though, was a huntress. The way Aunt Mary had talked about her, she was a fierce one. Uncle Declan was a jock. What made him so much more intimidating than Aunt Star? That was one of those things that Gam would say, "You have to live it to understand it."

Everyone laughed and carried on like it was the funniest thing to happen all year. If anything could be said of the Clauses, they were a jolly bunch.

The next day, Noel went with Shepherd and their parents to visit Noah and Lorelei. Noah had promised Noel and Shepherd that the next time they were down he would take them to see the animals. Dad almost balked at the idea; instead, he made Noah promise to visit calm, harmless animals. Parents could be over protective sometimes, but who cares? Animals were animals, and Noel loved animals. Honestly though, they had a pet polar bear. How much worse could it get?

"You just keep growing so much," Lorelei gushed. "You're both practically grown."

There were hugs all around, and then Mom asked about the elephant in the room just like she always does. "How is Ethan?"

"He's doing good," Noah answered.

"Don't lie, Uncle Noah," came a vaguely familiar voice from the back of the house. "He's still a bigot."

"Kellen, does your dad know where you are," Noah asked as Kellen walked into the living room where everyone was standing.

Kellen shrugged.

Noah looked at Lorelei with concern in his eyes and asked, "Did you tell Ethan Wynter's family was coming today?"

"No, I assumed you would do that," she answered.

"Why tell him? All he'll do is scowl a lot and forbid me from coming over here for the foreseeable future. What's the point?" Kellen asked. "Besides he doesn't know where I am anyway."

"Where does he think you are?" Lorelei asked.

"Practice... What? It got cancelled."

"The point is the consequences will be far worse if he finds out," Noah told his nephew.

"I don't really care. I thought you said you were working today. I went by the ranger station, and they said you weren't coming in," Kellen's tone sounded almost accusing.

"I said I was going to visit the animals. I didn't necessarily say I was working."

"Same thing."

"Not really, I'm taking Wynter's kids to see the animals. I just didn't want to mention that in front of Ethan."

"Oh."

"You're Ethan's son?" Mom asked with this sort of wonder filled voice. She had never met Kellen. All she'd ever seen were pictures; in fact, Noah had not even told Mom Kellen existed until he was five years old. Noel didn't remember that. She'd been too young herself, but she had heard Mom talk about it. Apparently, Ethan already had a son when he attempted his attack on the North Pole.

"Yeah, so?" Kellen nodded once to Shepherd, some kind of guy speak. Then he looked Noel's way and said, "You were pretty good the other day, Clause."

Clause? Like that was her whole name? That was just great that was probably all he saw when he looked at her. A Clause.

"Wait. The other day?" Noah inquired.

"Yeah, she was at the rink the other day when I had my lesson with Coach Declan."

"You look just like your dad," Mom marveled as if it didn't happen every day that kids look like their parents.

"I'm not anything like that man!" Kellen spit.

"Kellen, did you tell your dad about the hockey lesson?" Noah continued his questioning.

"What? Like I'm stupid or something? No, I didn't tell him. So, are we going to see the animals or not?"

"We are," Noah said indicating himself and the others. "You are going home."

"Nope, I never go home this early. Today I decided to tag along with you."

"I don't think that's a good idea," Lorelei inserted.

"Neither is going home, so which animals are we visiting?"

"Kellen if your dad finds out…" Noah sighed and answered, "Penguins."

"Excellent. I'll get the sardines."

"You've done this before," Mom smiled.

"I spend most of my time with Uncle Noah or playing hockey," Kellen mumbled as he disappeared further into the house.

"He and Ethan don't always see eye to eye, but he really is a good kid," Lorelei felt the need to defend.

Yeah, good and arrogant.

"Ready." Kellen led the way outside as if he were the South Pole ranger instead of his Uncle.

It felt like they had been walking forever when Noah came to a dead halt and put his arm out to stop everyone else. Noel was behind Shepherd, who at fifteen was already taller than Noel by several inches. He was going to be one big boy. She knew something was wrong when Shepherd stiffened and Dad pulled her back against his chest.

"What is it?" Noel whispered.

"Just back up very slowly," Noah instructed.

That was when Noel heard a soft whining sound. She pulled away from Dad just enough to peak around Shepherd. Curled up on the ground was a baby polar bear crying next to a much larger much deader polar bear.

"Oh no!" Noel gasped and rushed to the bear's side.

"Stop Noel!" Dad shouted, but Noel kept going.

She sat down in the snow and pulled the baby bear into her lap. The baby kept crying, so Noel pushed her head against the baby's head and forced magic through the baby bear's mind so that it could understand. "Shh, I've got you. Everything is going to be alright."

Kellen's eyes were as big as saucers. He asked, "Uncle Noah, is the mother dead?"

Noah did something, maybe checked for a pulse before answering. "Yeah."

"Mom, do something," Noel insisted.

"I can't," Mom said softly.

"Dad, please," Noel begged.

"Baby, I can't either."

Then Noel's annoying baby brother sat down next to her, put a hand on her back and said, "Noel, dead is dead. She's not hurt. She's gone, and it's too late for anyone to do anything. Not even your big heart can save her now."

Noel pulled the bear into a bear hug, and they cried together.

After a couple minutes, she looked up to see six set of eyes on her. Three looked somewhat shocked and terrified, and three looked sympathetic.

"Do you know that you're cuddling with a ferocious beast?" Kellen asked.

"Yeah, real ferocious. Besides, she needs a friend right now," Noel pointed out.

"She's too much like her mother," Dad sighed aggrieved.

"I tried to tell you," Shepherd said as he pushed back to his feet. "Noel is emotional. She's not going to deal."

They had been talking about her? Didn't matter. Right now, Noel was too busy making kissy faces at the baby bear to worry about her family.

"There, see. You're not so alone after all. Are you, princess?"

"Princess," Kellen choked.

"She's a girl. Why not princess?"

"Sure, why not? You're the polar bear whisperer. You can call her whatever you want."

The penguins forgotten, Noel was content to play with Princess the rest of the day while Shepherd and Dad helped Noah dispose of the body, and Kellen seemed satisfied to sit and watch Noel and Princess wrestling.

## Chapter Six

Noel was up early the next day. She ate quickly and asked Mom for permission to go find Princess.

"I don't know, Noel. Your dad won't like it," Mom said.

"Princess won't hurt me. I've lived my whole life with Roscoe, and he's a lot bigger than a little orphaned cub."

"I know. You're growing up and can handle yourself better than your dad thinks. Straight there, and straight back. Leave the other animals a wide birth."

"Yea, love you, Mom," Noel called over her shoulder already on her way out the door.

Noel went straight to the spot where they had first found Princess just like Mom had instructed. There was no lingering sign that a tragedy had taken place there. Fresh fallen snow had long since covered any trace of blood left from the mother bear.

Princess wasn't anywhere to be seen, but then she wouldn't survive well sitting out in the open. Noel started searching the area and nearly jumped out of her skin when the silence was broken.

"Does Uncle Noah know you're out here?" Kellen asked appearing from out of nowhere.

"Does he know where you are?" Noel turned the question back on him.

"Nah, but I'm not the one out looking for a natural predator."

"She's a baby, and she's all alone."

"You don't know she's alone."

"Most likely she's alone. I just wanted to make sure she was ok. Now, if you'll excuse me."

Kellen didn't leave; instead, he joined in the search. "How did you do that yesterday?" he asked after a while.

"Do what?"

"You calmed that bear like you could really speak to her or something."

"I could. Well, it isn't two way obviously, but she could understand me. We have a polar back home like that."

"I think I've heard Uncle Noah and Aunt Lorelei talk about that before, but I thought they were just yanking my chain."

"Nope, Roscoe is very real."

"Roscoe?"

"That's his name."

"And, you play with him the way you did that baby yesterday?"

"Sure, I've played with him all my life."

"I think I found something."

"Is it Princess?" Noel asked excitedly. She was getting her hopes up. The odds of survival for Princess were not good, especially now that she was motherless. At least Noah knew about her. That meant she was on the rangers' radar, and they would look out for her.

"I don't know. It looks like a den. We can't go in there," Kellen said throwing his arm up in front of

Noel. "You don't know what's in there. You don't go marching into a wild animal's den, and if you don't know any better than that, then you shouldn't be out here."

"Who died and made you king of the South? I can guarantee you that nothing inside that den is a match for my magic."

"Is that how you did it then? You used magic to connect with her yesterday?"

"Yes."

"Can she understand anyone?"

"Yes."

"How long will it last?"

"For life. Are you always this full of questions?"

"Your life or her life?"

"Her life?"

"I don't know much about Clause magic. I only know your family from afar."

"Because your dad hates us?"

"Yes."

"Why?"

"My grandmother says it isn't hate; it's hurt. Sometimes I think she's trying to convince herself of that instead of me. Uncle Noah says things are complicated. From my viewpoint, it's simple bigotry."

"You don't feel the same?"

"No. everyone loves Star Clause. From what I can tell her kids are all ok. Coach Declan married her, so she can't be all bad, right? That little boy of theirs has skill. He's already a good little hockey player. Under Coach Declan's tutelage, he could leave here and go pro."

"What if he doesn't want to leave here?" Noel challenged.

Kellen shrugged but didn't have much to say to that.

Noel fell to her knees in the snow outside the opening to the den and called, "Princess?"

Within seconds a very small polar bear was charging eagerly into Noel's arms.

"I guess we found her," Kellen commented drily.

Princess ran through the entrance to the den and back to Noel before running inside the den again. Noel stood up and moved to follow.

"What are you doing, Clause?" Kellen exclaimed.

"She wants me to follow."

"This isn't a good idea," he mumbled as he followed behind Noel.

Who asked him to follow anyway. If it was such a bad idea, he was welcome to go back home.

Princess was alone in the den, and Noel was hit with the magnitude of the loneliness. She couldn't imagine Roscoe spending any significant amount of time alone without going crazy. Poor Princess, all alone last night in this big scary world. Noel sat down and settled Princess into her lap.

"Do you think she ate anything?" Noel asked.

Kellen shrugged, "How should I know?"

"She's so young." She couldn't have been more than a few months old. Any polar bear that fit easily into Noel's lap, couldn't possibly be very old.

"Will she let me touch her?" Kellen asked.

"How should I know?" Noel threw his earlier words back in his face.

Slowly tentatively Kellen moved closer and extended his arm. He ran his hand gently over

Princess's head and down her back. "Wow," Kellen breathed.

Kellen's wonder filled face betrayed his excitement. He was smiling even, and he had a wonderful smile. Impossibly, it made him look so much better, and he looked good enough before he started to smile. Noel decided that Kellen should smile more. Besides the fact that it looked good on him, it made him appear more approachable. Everything about him seemed a little friendlier when he smiled. Petting Princess, Kellen's face glowed with barely contained joy. It was what Noel imagined children all around the world must look like on Christmas morning when they realized Santa had been there.

Noel ideally wondered if that was how she was the first time she met Roscoe. She was too young to remember it of course. She wondered how an infant would react to seeing a fully grown male polar bear.

Noel and Kellen had been there for roughly twenty minutes when Princess began to whine. Noel nuzzled her neck making shushing noises while Kellen scratched behind her ears. Princess wiggled her head around to suck on Kellen's thumb before she started to whine again.

"What's wrong with her?" Kellen asked.

"I'm not sure. Maybe she's hungry."

"Do you think she knows how to hunt yet?"

"Doesn't look like it."

"We could go get Uncle Noah," Kellen suggested.

Noel nodded. "Hurry back."

"You're not staying here alone."

"I'm not leaving Princess here alone."

Kellen pulled a phone from his pocket. "No signal," he sighed. "I still don't like the idea of leaving you out here alone. You never should have been out here alone to start with."

"My mom knew I was coming, and last time I checked, you weren't her. I can handle myself." As demonstration, Noel used magic to form and levitate a good-sized snowball. Then she exploded the snowball covering herself, Kellen, and Princess in cold, wet slush. "And, that was child's play compared to what I will do if attacked. Now, hurry up and go get Noah."

Kellen was gone for what felt like forever while Noel sat with a pitifully hungry baby polar. Princess was miserable, and that was making Noel miserable.

Kellen didn't want to leave them alone earlier; where was he now? What was taking him so long?

"Clause?" Kellen called from the mouth of the cave.

"Hurry up and get in here!" Noel responded more than a little miffed.

Kellen walked into the den holding three large bottles of milk and no Noah in sight.

"Where's Noah?"

"He was working and couldn't come. That's what took me so long. He gave me directions, and I had to fix the bottles myself."

"Did you do it right?" Noel worried.

"I guess we'll find out. Uncle Noah said that she might not drink it all this first time since it's not mother's milk. He said she'd get the hang of it though, and she has to be fed several times daily."

Noel took one of the bottles from Kellen and poked the nipple in Princess's mouth. "Drink it. It's good for you."

Princess did just as she was told. Kellen watched in wonderment as Princess downed all three bottles, and

Noel cooed at Princess until the cub nodded off
to sleep.

Noel returned twice more that day to feed Princess.
The bear's spirit was up. She was in a visibly better
mood and more playful. It really was a shame that
Princess didn't have any siblings to keep her company.
It broke Noel's heart to leave Princess alone each time.

## Chapter Seven

Noel had just returned from giving Princess her evening bottles when Uncle Joseph suddenly appeared right dab in the middle of Aunt Star's living room. He arrived with a very terrorized looking woman.

Aunt Heidi shrieked when they appeared. "Oh! I don't think I'll ever get used to that! Honestly, would it kill this family to use the door like normal people?"

Noel couldn't help a smile at Aunt Heidi. She had been a part of the Clause family longer than she ever lived with her own family. She used her own fair share of teleportation magic too.

After Aunt Heidi took a couple of deep calming breaths, the room fell into a disquieted silence. Everyone was staring at the woman who had come along for the ride. It was hard not to. Noel didn't know for sure if everyone felt the same as she did, but she couldn't look away because the new visitor was too stunning to miss. She had an absolute natural beauty that captured your attention.

She had copper colored hair. Not red, not orange, not auburn, but copper. Her eyes were as green as a freshly cut lawn, not that you ever saw any in the North or South Poles. She had lashes longer and fuller than any one person has a right to. Pale skin as flawless as the porcelain dolls that sat on Noel's shelves at home meant to look pretty. There was a smattering of freckles across her cheek bones that only served to give her a more innocent look. She was short in a dainty feminine sort of way.

More of her was covered than was not. She had on a full length, black maxi dress with three quarter length sleeves and a slit on the right side up to her knee. It was a perfectly modest dress, and yet it showed off her very powerful assets. She had curves in all the right places just like Aunt Star. Her rounded rear end was plumb without being fat. She had a butt that could put even Aunt Marci's to shame.

She had on very little makeup, and she didn't need it. There was a natural rose to her cheeks and her full to be envied lips. All she needed was a nun's habit to be the world's most provocative nun. No offence or anything, but seriously, what was this girl doing with Uncle Joseph?

"Lucy?" Uncle Joseph queried breaking the silence.

The woman, apparently named Lucy, made a sound that more so resembled a wounded animal than anything human.

Uncle Joseph only had eyes for Lucy. His gaze was fixated on her, and he hadn't looked anywhere else. "Are you ok?" he asked.

"No, I don't think so," Lucy deadpanned.

"Do you want me to take you home?" Uncle Joseph asked her.

"Yes, please."

And, just like that they disappeared as quickly as they had appeared. For a long time, no one uttered a word.

"Does someone want to tell me what that was all about?" Uncle North asked. He looked at each of his siblings in turn, but none said a thing. Papa was the oldest, but Uncle North had always played the role of oldest. Noel didn't understand the dynamics behind it, and she had never asked.

Uncle North pinned Aunt Mary with a stern stare. "Mary, who was that with him?"

"Lucy," Aunt Mary answered smartly.

"You mean to tell me that out of everyone in this room, no one knows what's going on with that boy?" Uncle North asked the room in general.

"Joseph hasn't been a boy for a long time. He's an adult who can take care of himself," Aunt Mary defended. Uncle Joseph and Aunt Mary were the two youngest of the six siblings, and they had always been close. That's why it was so surprising that Uncle Joseph would just show up like that without Aunt Mary expecting him and with someone Aunt Mary had never heard anything about.

"Well, where is he these days?" Uncle North asked. How much you want to bet Uncle North would keep a closer tab on his five siblings after that?

"Last I talked to him he was working out of France." Aunt Mary was the only one to answer, the only one to know anything at all about Uncle Joseph's whereabouts.

"That wasn't French they were speaking," Uncle Israel pointed out. "I'd say he's moved on again."

That wasn't entirely surprising. Uncle Joseph tended to get bored easier than the others and move about more in the hunt. Still, Noel would have thought someone would have known where he had moved last. He wouldn't be on Dad's radar for the naughty and nice list, but maybe Dad had gotten a feel for which direction Joseph had gone last.

Noel looked at her dad. Nope, he looked just as lost as anyone else. Huh, weird. It was almost like Uncle Joseph was hiding from family, but if that were the case, he wouldn't have shown up in the middle of Aunt Star's living room like that. He had to know everyone was here. They had been planning this week since Noel's birthday last year. It was a good time for Dad and Papa to get away, having just finished the big Christmas Eve run.

"Do you think I scared her off?" Aunt Marci asked with a quivering lip.

"Of course not, baby doll. That girl already looked like a cornered doe," Uncle North told his wife with a tender voice and gently kissed her. No one could pull out Uncle North's soft side like Aunt Marci.

"Why doesn't someone just call him?" Shepherd asked as if should have been the most obvious answer ever. Noel agreed with her brother.

"Joseph doesn't keep a sat phone on him, Shep," Aunt Mary answered. She always called Shepherd Shep. So, did Uncle Joseph. They were the only two who ever did. Shepherd didn't seem to mind. He was just that easy going. It was another trait that would serve him well when he took over the job of Santa someday.

"Why not?" Kris wanted to know.

"He doesn't like the bulk of it," Aunt Mary explained.

"It's just lazy is what it is," Peace said. He didn't live up to his name most times. He had a short fuse and a horrid temper.

"Is he ok? Do you think?" Aunt Star asked. There was a tone of desperation in her voice that caused Noel to look up and take stock of the room. All the adults looked worried.

"He didn't look like he was in distress," Dad told them all. "Lucy, on the other hand, looked very distressed. Joseph was clearly worried about her, but he looked fine himself."

"He'll still have questions to answer," Uncle North announced.

"Lucy Sanders," Papa said unexpectedly. "I remember her. Sweet girl. Never on the naughty list. Yes, a good Christian girl. I wonder what that was all about."

Noel loved that about Papa. He identified with the girl, and he was just as concerned about Lucy as he was Joseph. Papa had enough love for everyone, not just family. Noel had even seen Papa fretting over the naughty list, because he loved them too, just as much. Papa was a good example for all of them on how God wants us to love others.

"I'm sure they're fine, dear," Gam assured Papa. "Lucy is a good girl, and Joseph is a smart, capable man."

"You're right!" Aunt Heidi quickly bandwagoned. "We're all sitting around worrying about nothing. They're fine, and I'm sure Joseph will bring her back around to meet us all when she's ready."

"Do you think he's dating her then?" Aunt Star perked up swiftly.

"That has to be it!" Bell chimed in. "Didn't you see how worried he was for her? She was the whole of his attention."

"Has Uncle Joseph ever brought a girl home to meet the family?" Carol asked.

"Never," Aunt Mary answered simply.

"He can't, can he? Not really," Yule said. He wasn't married either. Come to think of it none of Uncle North's grandkids were married. They were all grown, but none married. "Bringing someone home to meet the family has to be the last step. Otherwise you would have people all across the world who knew about the Clauses."

He had a valid point. One that Noel would like to hear the response to before she got out there.

"Do you think he's serious about this one?" Hope asked with a big smile.

Yule shrugged. "Don't know. He didn't exactly introduce her, did he, and with Uncle Joseph that could mean anything."

That was true too. Noel thought Yule was on a roll.

"Whatever the situation, Joseph appeared unhurt. In the meantime, we all need to do a better job keeping in touch with Joseph. It isn't right, that no one knows anything," Uncle North lectured bringing the whole conversation to an end.

For the rest of the evening, Noel waited thinking that surely Uncle Joseph would show back up with Lucy, but it didn't happen. Uncle Joseph was such an enigma.

# Chapter Eight

By the next day it had become routine for Noel to pick up milk bottles on her way out to feed Princess. No one else was interested in going. They had seen polar bears before, they said. It was quiet, peaceful out that far from town. Not many people ventured that far. Mostly only rangers would wander that far, and they were trained to be unobtrusive.

When she got to the den, Kellen was already there. What was he doing there? Was he following her? Because, if so, that was uncomfortable to say the least.

"What are you doing here?" There was an attitude to her voice that Noel had not meant to put, but this guy was making her uncomfortable.

"I had time to kill before practice. Usually I'll tag along with Uncle Noah, but he's dealing with human exploders today. I figured I'd come watch you feed Princess instead."

"And, you don't think that's weird?"

"Nah, I like animals. I think she's hungry," Kellen said indicating the cub in his lap. Princess had bonded with him it seemed.

Noel sat down and took Princess to feed her the first of her bottles. "I'm only here for a week."

"I didn't think that many Clauses would move into Mrs. Star's place permanently."

Smart aleck. "Someone will need to feed Princess when I'm gone."

"That's the ranger's job. It's what they do."

"I know that, but she knows you already. She likes you."

Kellen looked Noel in the eyes for a brief moment before responding. "Aright, I can play mommy to the little monster."

"She's not a monster!" Noel said taken aback.

"Yeah, she is. She was trying to eat through my favorite pair of jeans before you got here. Weren't you, you little monster?" Kellen ruffled the fur on

Princess's face causing her to abandon the bottle temporarily while she wrestled with him.

After a couple minutes, Kellen disentangled himself from Princess's grasp and said, "I've got to get to practice. Later, Clause. Princess, you be good.

Now that was taken care of, Noel could relax and enjoy the rest of her week in the South Pole. Uncle Joseph didn't show again. It was strange. Noel was actually starting to worry about the man too. What was going on with Uncle Joseph? Who was that girl to him, and why did she look so scared?

"Papa, do you think Uncle Joseph is ok?" Noel finally asked one afternoon. Gloria and Angel's eyes focused in on Papa too. They wanted an answer to that question as badly as Noel. Uncle Joseph was far from predictable, but this was… different.

Papa laid a finger aside of his nose; it was an inside joke based on that silly poem the humans were so fond of. Noel had never told anyone, but she liked it too.

Then he winked and said, "Oh, I wouldn't worry about Joseph too much."

"Uncle Bubba, did you use some of your Santa mojo to spy on Uncle Joseph?" Gloria accused.

"Would I do that?" Papa grinned.

Angel wrapped her arms around Papa's neck. "Thank you!"

"There now, the Clauses look out for family," Papa said. "You girls quit worrying and have a little fun while we're all here."

That was exactly what the girls did too. They enjoyed every moment to the fullest. The night of the dance, the girls began early in the afternoon doing each other's hair and makeup. Joy sat on the bed watching most of the day, because Uncle Declan had decreed that she was too young to wear makeup.

She cheered right up, though, when Noel promised her, "We'll do your hair. Uncle Declan didn't say anything about your hair, and we know he won't make you go bald headed."

Joy laughed infectiously at that one, and soon all four girls were rolling on the floor laughing.

Eventually, all four had an up-do, simple, elegant, and gorgeous.

"You girls ready to go?" Mom asked poking her head in the door. "Don't you girls look beautiful."

"Daddy wouldn't let me wear makeup," Joy announced in an accusing tone.

"You don't need it. You have a classic beauty that's all your own," Mom assured her. After Mom's assurance, Joy's face lit with a glow that was beautiful and mesmerizing.

The dance was amazing. Aunt Star had rented out the town's largest meeting hall. It was even larger than Uncle Declan's ice rink. The decorations were magical, literally. A slight snowfall fell all around them disappearing as it hit the ground. The ceiling sparkled like the starry night sky. A punch fountain was set up in one corner and a fondue fountain in the opposite corner. There was food galore, soft lighting, and good music.

All the Clauses looked beautiful, and so did the rest of the town. The place was packed. It sort of made Noel feel like a sardine. There was so much open space in the North Pole. In that meeting hall that night, there was hardly elbow room. Nevertheless, somehow people found room to dance. Noel danced with her dad, with Papa, and even one song with Shepherd. Mostly the girls danced together.

"Your mother's first birthday after we met was the first time I ever danced with her," Dad told. Noel had heard the story a million times.

"Yeah, I know. You couldn't look away, and you should have known in that moment that you were in love with her."

"That's right, smarty pants. We still dance every year on her birthday, and now I get the pleasure of dancing with you on your birthday too."

"You don't dance with Shepherd on his birthday," Noel pointed out with a mischievous grin.

He twirled her into a spin that was so fast she crashed against his chest. "Dad!" she laughed.

"I like our birthday dances," Noel admitted.

"Me too, sweetheart. Me too." As the song ended, Dad kissed the top of her head and let her pull away.

"Do I get a dance?" Papa asked.

"Of course," Noel smiled.

Papa wasn't as good a dancer as Dad, but he was fun. He knew how to laugh at his own mistakes, and he made Noel laugh too. Dancing with Dad was special, because it was such a tender and emotional moment. Dancing with Papa was fun.

A fast song started, and Noel cackled as Papa started shimmying across the dance floor with her in tow. He kind of resembled a confused peacock, but he sure looked handsome in his red vested tuxedo.

"Come on," Gloria said after Noel's dance with Papa. "I need some space. I'm not used to this closeness."

Angel and Noel followed Gloria outside and around the building. "That's a lot of people in a little space," Gloria complained.

"It's fun, like a guilty pleasure," Noel smiled.

"Our dances are always like that. Someone needs to petition to get a new dance hall built. Somewhere that is big enough to hold one of the town dances especially for town dances," Angel described.

"Do you have that many dances?" Gloria asked.

"You're kidding, right? You have met my Mom."

The girls turned a corner and nearly ran over Kellen Nickola. He was dressed in a thick coat over his long-sleeved T-shirt and a pair of ratty old jeans. Noel was pretty sure they were the same pair that he accused Princess of trying to put a hole in only days ago. It really was disappointing after seeing all the other guys dressed to the tee in tuxes. Kellen Nicola would have rocked a tux too. Too bad.

"I know that isn't what Aunt Star gave you to wear tonight," Noel called him out.

"Mrs. Star didn't give me an outfit for tonight."

"Why wouldn't she? That doesn't sound like Aunt Star," Gloria replied.

"He never comes to any of the dances," Angel supplied while Kellen studied his boots.

"Why not?" Gloria asked, but Noel was just about sure she saw where this was going.

"My dad won't let me."

"Talk about over protective. What does he think is going to happen? The whole town is here. You're more likely to get in trouble not coming to the dance."

"Aren't you afraid someone will see you and tell your dad?" Noel asked softly feeling sorry for him.

Kellen looked Noel right in her eyes and asked, "Are you going to tell him?"

"Me? No. He wouldn't listen to us anyway. Clauses, remember?"

"Yeah, I remember. How's Princess?"

"Good."

There was something different about Kellen standing outside in the moonlight. His smile. He wasn't smiling. Noel supposed there was nothing to smile about standing outside a dance you aren't allowed to join. Kellen without his smile was like a cake without icing. It still looks delicious, but it would look so much better complete.

"Good… I um, I better go," Kellen mumbled.

"That's so sad," Gloria voiced.

"What is?" Angel was clueless.

"Kellen Nickola."

"What is so sad about him?"

"Angel, what do you think he was doing hanging out here?"

"Lurking."

"Look," Gloria pointed to the window they were standing next to. "He was watching. The whole town is here, and he isn't allowed to come."

"Oh, you think he was spying, because he's jealous."

"Yes."

It was sad, but what could any of them do about it. If Kellen's dad wouldn't listen to Mom, he sure wouldn't listen to any of them.

"Who's jealous?" Shepherd asked rounding the corner.

"Kellen Nickola. His dad doesn't let him come to any of the dances even though the rest of the town does. His dad doesn't like our family, so Kellen gets left out," Angel quickly spilled. Noel loved Angel, but that girl would be lousy with confidential information.

"Mmm. It's not like the North Pole in there, is it?" Shepherd said.

"It's a nice change of pace," Noel replied.

"Yeah, want to dance?" he asked Noel.

"Sure." She followed Shepherd back inside and out to the dance floor. Dad had taught Shepherd how to dance from a very young age. As a result, he was an eloquent dancer just like Dad.

"Are you hanging out with him now?" Shepherd asked. He didn't say who, but he was talking about Kellen.

"Nah, not really. I've just seen him around a couple times." It wasn't any of Shepherd's business. Noel didn't know why he would care anyway.

"Be careful. His dad really doesn't like Mom. There's no telling what he's capable of."

"That's his dad, not Kellen. He's actually not that bad." Noel genuinely believed Kellen said he wasn't like his dad.

"Still, it's not a good idea to become too familiar with Kellen Nickola. I just want you to be safe."

## Chapter Nine

Noel didn't want to go back home and not just because she would miss everyone else, which she would. She didn't want to go back, because her future was waiting on her back home.

No one said anything about Noel's future the first day back home or even the second. Unpacking and settling back into a routine seemed to be more important for now, but Noel knew it wouldn't last.

It was the third day back when they sat down to eat dinner that Dad said, "Noel, have you given any more thought about what we said, about your future?"

"I have given it a lot of thought, and I still feel the same. Would you want me to go out and kill innocents?"

"These are not innocents that we are talking about. We're talking about vampires, monsters, killers. They kill innocents every single day by draining their victim dry. You're trying to make light of it, but it is a war. The humans have no idea who they're up against or even that they are under attack. Would you want to have those humans' blood on your hands when you could have done something to save them but chose not to?"

"I'm not responsible for their actions, only my own."

"Noel, it is a family tradition," Mom said softly.

"Maybe it's time to start a new tradition."

"What sort of new tradition? Clauses fight vampires for the humans' benefit. Isn't the job of Santa for the humans' benefit as well? If we stop one tradition, why not stop them all? We'd certainly have more time on our hands."

"What about you, Mom? I don't see you running out to join the war on vampires."

"That was different. I was an only child."

"So, what you're saying is that it is Shepherd's fault you're trying to force me to do something I feel is morally wrong, or is it your fault for not stopping after one child?"

"Noel!" Mom gasped. She was mad. Her face was bright red, and her eyes were wide. Good. Noel was mad too. Noel slammed her fork to the table, pushed to her feet, and retreated to her room.

Noel couldn't stand to look at her mom. She was such a hypocrite. She wanted Noel to be this perfect little daughter who does exactly as she's told. That's not what Mom did when she was young. She was older than Noel was now when she ran away.

Breakfast was quiet. Everyone had eaten at different times then run off to get chores done. It took a lot to keep the North Pole running. Noel had always done her fair share to help, but that wasn't good enough she supposed. Mom and Dad still wanted her gone.

After rinsing her dishes and putting them into the dishwasher, Noel left out to feed Roscoe and the reindeer.

Roscoe was first. His favorite food was seal, but he had become very domesticated over the years. He would turn his nose up if you offered him raw meat. He much preferred his seal cooked. Once upon a time, he only got cooked seal as a treat on special occasions, but he was so old now and feeble, no one had the heart to tell him no. They all knew it was only a matter of time before they lost him. For now, they just wanted him to be happy.

Dad had built a large firepit for the explicit purpose of cooking Roscoe's food and a refrigerated storage building for stockpiling his seal meat.

Noel snuggled Roscoe's neck and asked, "Are you hungry?"

She opened the storage door and used magic to heft one of the seal carcasses onto the firepit. Thank heavens Roscoe still enjoyed pulling the meat from the bones himself. Noel couldn't imagine having to de-bone and dress the carcasses. They were gross enough as is.

Noel started a roaring fire to cook the meat, and she sat down next to Roscoe to wait. He was so much bigger than she was. It was hard to imagine that he was getting weaker. He had always been larger than life. He was her best friend, and she was losing him. That thought alone hurt bad enough, but what if she were gone somewhere killing when they lost him? Would he understand that she didn't abandon him, that she still loved him?

She buried her face in Roscoe's fur as tears leaked from her eyes. "I love you, Roscoe," she mumbled.

He bent his head and nuzzled her in return. They sat there in the cold snow together until the smell of cooked seal reminded Noel of what she still had to do. She laid the seal in front of Roscoe and put out the fire.

"I'll see you later big boy. I've got to go feed the reindeer now."

Roscoe nudged her shoulder before digging into his seal.

"You're welcome," Noel laughed.

Out in the stable, Noel dumped oats into each stall quickly. The reindeer were good eaters, and they knew from routine that the sooner they finished their food the sooner Noel would take them out to stretch their legs.

Once everyone was finished, Noel opened the stall gates. Donner and Dancer were the first two out. They were the youngest, and it showed. Donner took off at a fast sprint. He would spend the whole morning running. Dancer, on the other hand, wasn't nearly that fast as she shook it across the ice. Yep, no joke. She shimmied her behind everywhere she went. Dancer was a bit of a show-off, but if Noel had moves like that, she'd probably show off too.

Prancer and Blitzen weren't far behind. Blitzen was jumping about today. You never really knew what Blitzen would do from day to day. She was so hyper. She made Noel laugh most of the time and always expect the unexpected. With Prancer, you knew exactly what you were going to get. Prancer was a skipper. He skipped everywhere he went. It was hilarious to watch.

Noel made a video of Dancer and Prancer once. Boy, did those two really ham it up for the camera. They were the North Pole's very own comedians.

Donner was gone out of sight by that point, but he'd be back. He ran, fast, everywhere he went, but he would always be back. He was the most reliable as well as the fastest. Those two qualities together were what made him a great leader.

Vixen was the next to pass Noel on her way out of the stable. Vixen huffed at Noel and kept walking without so much as looking in Noel's direction. It wasn't anything personal. Vixen was simply boy crazy.

She had very little use for girls. Papa had been her favorite person until Dad had showed up, and Dad had been her favorite until Shepherd was born. More than she liked boys, she loved to cuddle. If Noel were to go after Vixen and wrap her in a hug, Vixen would be more than happy to spend some quality cuddle time, and Noel would later.

Cupid was the next one out. He slowed up just enough to bump Noel's shoulder with his head. Not that he was moving very fast to begin with. Cupid was getting old. This year would most likely be his last Christmas Eve run. There were some young fawns ready to come up, but it would surely break Cupid's heart when he was retired.

The last two out were Comet and Dasher, the slow pokes. They even let the old man beat them out of the stable. "Alright, you two get a move on," Noel yelled at them. Then she approached them and gave them a swift pop to the behind.

She wasn't trying to be mean, but you had to keep a firm hand with Comet and Dasher. They were lazy and would try anything to get out of exercise. They both snorted their displeasure at being slapped so undignified like. Once they were finally out of the stable, Noel took off chasing after them. It was about the only way to get those two moving on a regular basis.

Noel chased after Comet and Dasher for most of an hour before returning to Vixen to give her a little love. When Noel hugged Vixen, Vixen nuzzled back so enthusiastically that she almost toppled Noel to the ground. Yeah, the flirt may have been boy crazy, but she would always have a soft spot in her heart for cuddling.

"Donner, let's go," Noel yelled, and Donner came running back into the opening. "Time to go back guys. Come on."

None of the reindeer put up a fuss about going back to their stalls this time. Sometimes Blitzen would, the hyper little thing.

Next stop were the young fawns. They would need more play time to stretch out and exercise their quickly growing bodies.

Noel's two favorites were Captain and Cookie. Captain was the oldest, and by all rights he should be the next one to move up the ranks. It wasn't going to happen though. Captain was good, but Noel had named him Captain for a reason. He was a natural leader. He and Donner would butt heads. When Donner got older, Captain would move up.

Cookie was the one set to move up into Cupid's position. Noel had named her too, because when she was younger and she would come out to visit the young fawns with her dad, Cookie was always stealing cookies right out of Dad's hand. She liked cookies almost as much as Dad. Noel didn't think there was a person or animal alive who liked cookies more than Dad.

The hardest part of exercising the fawns was keeping them rounded up. They couldn't be trusted out on their own like Donner could. Donner always found his way back and came when he was called. The fawns, not so much. That had been a frustrating lesson to learn.

Part of Noel's job with the fawns was to teach them to follow commands. That was a lot harder than it sounded, and it didn't sound all that easy. Reindeer could be a stubborn lot. All the fawns were interested in was playing. In a way, it wasn't entirely fair. The sleigh team did get to play when they got out, but they had been following commands a lot more years than Noel had been alive.

Reindeer training took a lot of patience, a lot of time, and a whole lot of determination. Sometimes the only thing you could do was out stubborn the reindeer, which was aggravating on the best of days.

Still, Noel was sure she had the better job. Shepherd had to help out in the toy shop with the elves. She didn't know how he ever got anything done. Always surrounded by toys and elves, Noel wouldn't do anything but play all day. Noel wouldn't want to be cooped up inside all day either.

Wonder why Mom and Dad were so intent on running her off? The job she did around here was just as important as the rest of them. Dad said it himself that the reindeer had been doing a much better job since Noel started a daily regiment with them, and Papa said that there hadn't been anyone working with the young fawns since he was a boy. Who would take her place if she were to travel the world killing vampires?

Chapter Ten

Noel managed to avoid everyone at lunch due to work. At dinner, she went up to Papa and Gam's house.

"I'm making spaghetti tonight. Why don't you stay for dinner?" Gam suggested, but then Noel had known that she would. Gam was always eager to feed everyone and have everyone sit down together to eat. "I'll call your mom to see if they'll come up."

It wasn't exactly avoiding Mom and Dad, but at least Mom and Dad wouldn't start an argument in front of Papa and Gam.

"Hey, Gam," Shepherd greeted as he walked through the kitchen.

"Don't go anywhere. Your parents are on the way up for spaghetti."

"Awesome, I love your spaghetti."

"I know you do."

"What are you up to?" Shepherd asked Noel.

"Nothing. How was the toy shop?" Noel inquired genuinely curious.

"Crazy. Someone slipped the elves some sugar cookies."

"Dad," they both laughed in unison.

Dad was the world's worst about giving the elves cookies. He says that when they do a good job they should be rewarded, and Dad's favorite reward was a sugar cookie. The problem was that sugar cookies didn't make Dad insanely hyper. The elves were like the most annoying creatures alive after a few sugar cookies.

"So, are we eating Gam's spaghetti to avoid a certain sore subject?"

Noel shrugged.

"It's brilliant. For what it's worth, I can't imagine the North Pole without you."

"What's that?" Gam asked as she pulled fresh garlic bread from the oven.

"Nothing," Noel lied.

"Young lady, I don't lie to you. Don't lie to me."

"She's arguing with Mom and Dad about vampire hunting," Shepherd ratted her out.

"That's dreadful. At least tonight will give everyone a break. Go and tell Papa it's time for dinner."

Papa was in his office. "Papa?"

"There's my girl. Come give Papa some love." Papa still referred to himself in third person often. It was a habit that Gam says he picked up when he was trying to teach Noel and Shepherd to say Papa.

Noel sat down on Papa's lap and wrapped her arms around his neck. "Gam said it's time for dinner."

"What's Gam got good to eat?"

"Spaghetti."

"Ah, it's a trick you know," Papa said.

"A trick how?"

"Gam knows it's Shepherds favorite, so anytime she thinks it has been too long since you all came up for a meal, she'll cook spaghetti."

"How did I not know that?"

"Your Gam is sneaky like that. You have to keep a close eye on her. Come on. Let's go get some grub."

By the time Papa and Noel got back to the kitchen everyone else was already at the table waiting to say the blessing.

"How was Cupid today?" Dad asked.

"Slow. He's still faster than Comet and Dasher," Noel reported.

"Is he still eating well?" Mom wanted to know.

"He is. He's a trooper. I don't know how much longer he can make the Christmas Eve run though."

"I thought he was going to retire after this next year," Gam interjected.

"He is," Dad replied. "He's done a good job and deserves to enjoy his retirement."

"How are the young fawns? Any ready to come up?" Papa asked.

"Captain and Cookie are both ready any time. I don't think Captain and Donner need to work together. They're both used to being in charge. Two dominants could cause problems."

"I don't know how you do it every day," Shepherd commented.

"What do you mean?" Mom asked Shepherd.

"Noel spends hours every single day in the freezing cold working with the fawns only to progress at a snail's pace. I can deal with the sleigh team, because they're more mature and already trained. If I had to deal with the fawns there wouldn't be any to join the sleigh team in the future."

Noel knew what he was doing, and she appreciated it. He was pointing out her usefulness and emphasizing what they'd all be losing if she left the North Pole.

"We've all got our talents," Dad agreed.

"I'm just glad her talent is with the reindeer."

"God gives us many talents, right?" Mom said elbowing Dad in the side.

Real smooth, Mom, Noel couldn't help thinking.

"Oh, yeah, He does."

That was the last that was said about talents or where talents could be used. There was no talk of a future further away than the next week, and there was certainly no talk about vampires or vampire hunting.

That night Mom caught Noel before she could rush off to bed. "Hold up, Noel."

"What's up?"

"Was that your doing at dinner tonight? Having your brother speak up on your behalf?"

"I honestly didn't put him up to anything. He did that all on his own."

"We still have to talk about this. I prefer that we talk about it calmly and rationally."

"Mom, I don't think I can. I'm too emotionally involved, and I don't know how to remove the emotions attached long enough to remain calm."

"Well, you're just going to have to figure it out. You're eighteen now. You're not a kid anymore. It's time for you to show a little maturity."

"That's nice coming from you. I'm at least sticking around to settle things. I didn't just run away when things got hard. You were a brat."

"Noel, that's enough," Dad boomed.

Noel turned on her heel. She barely made it back to her room before the torrential down pour of tears began. She threw herself on her bed and cried herself to sleep.

The next morning, Shepherd was up early and in the kitchen when Noel came down for breakfast.

"That was really low what you did last night," Shepherd accused with no preamble.

"What would you know about it? You're not the one being booted out of the North Pole."

"No, I'm not, but my future was decided for me. You act like you're the only one who has to live up to family tradition. Poor, pitiful Noel. News flash, Noel, you're not alone, and you're not the only one hurting either. You made Mom cry last night. Why are you lashing out at her anyway?"

"I was only reacting to her."

"Is that what you think? You think Mom wants to let her little girl go? You think Mom wants you hunting vampires? You've heard the story. Mom was Dad's biggest advocate. She was the one who fought to save him. Mom believes in redemption. Mom isn't the one who wants you to follow family tradition. Mom is only backing Dad on this one, but you were the brat last night."

Shepherd said his peace then left Noel standing alone in the kitchen. Alone and confused.

That day after her chores were done, Noel went back for Roscoe, and the two walked out far enough that the others would leave them alone. Noel needed room to think, and she couldn't do that with everyone breathing down her neck. Nothing made sense anymore.

Roscoe and Noel didn't return home until after eight that night. Noel hadn't figured anything out when they returned. She wasn't any closer to making sense of things than when she left.

"Noel, where have you been?" Mom asked immediately as Noel walked in the back door.

"I was out with Roscoe," Noel answered and kept moving. She went straight upstairs to her room and shut the door.

She was already dressed for bed when Dad knocked on the door and walked in. He shut the door then sat down on the bed and patted the spot next to him. "We need to talk."

Noel sat down and waited, yet Dad didn't start talking.

"What did you want to talk about?"

"Your behavior last night was entirely inappropriate. What you said to your mom was out of line."

"I know. I'll apologize to her. Is that all?"

"No, that's not all… There's something I need you to understand. I've seen the carnage vampires can cause. I've seen the pain and hurt they can cause. I'm not talking about just the physical, Noel. I'm talking about emotional pain and unrest. I didn't think Aunt Mary would ever forgive me. I wouldn't have blamed her if she didn't. I had a lot harder time forgiving myself."

Noel wasn't sure what Dad was talking about, but it was a moot point. He was forgiven. "Dad, that's why I don't want to do this. It isn't right. What if there are more out there who need help?"

"What will you do for them, Noel? Will you marry them all? You know that's the only way your Mom could have helped me."

"But, Dad-"

"No, Noel. I've talked to Aunt Mary and Aunt Star, and your Mom is backing me on this. You're going to the South Pole where Aunt Mary and Aunt Star have agreed to train you. When you're finished training, if you still don't think you can do it... Well, we'll figure something out. I feel very strongly about this. If all the Clauses just quit hunting vampires, where does that leave the world?"

"Dad–"

"No. This is the end of the discussion for now. The least you can do is train and give it some thought." Dad got up and walked back to the door. "Pack up. You leave in the morning," was the last thing Dad said.

Chapter Eleven

Noel told Dad at breakfast that she could get herself to the South Pole. It was true. She had mastered transportation as a preteen, but that wasn't the point. If he wanted her to grow up and take responsibility for herself, that was exactly what she would do, and stepping out on her own meant she no longer needed Daddy to hold her hand. The slight stung. She could see it on his face.

All morning long, Noel hemmed and hawed around, taking her time. It was nearly lunch time before she was packed and ready to go.

"Noel?" Mom called softly from the door. She didn't say anything else, but her eyes were red.

Noel moved across the room hugged Mom close, not ready to let go.

"I love you," Mom whispered.

"I love you too."

"Promise me you'll be careful."

"I will. How long will I be there?"

"I don't know, baby."

"Will you come to visit me?"

"Sure. Dad will too and Shepherd."

Noel nodded, too choked up to trust her voice. It was hitting her finally that she was leaving home, and she had no idea for how long. She hadn't been away from home for more than a few days at a time, maybe a week, and she had never been away from her family. She hadn't grown up like most children having sleep overs or going to camp. She hadn't even left her mom to go to school each day. Mom was her teacher.

"I'm scared," Noel said breathlessly.

"Me too," Mom admitted pulling back enough to look Noel in the face. Mom started smoothing her wild curls away from her face and said, "You're all grown up now. Everything is going to be ok. As much as I want to be there, I can't, but Aunt Mary and Aunt Star are going to look out for you. This will be good for you, we'll see." Then she kissed the top of Noel's head.

Noel loved that Mom had said we'll see, not you'll see. It helped Noel not to feel so much alone in this. Mom was looking for the silver lining too, yet she believed that somehow it would all turn out for the best. "You ready to go, sweetheart?"

Noel nodded. She took a deep breath. "Bye, Mom." With that, Noel transported herself and her luggage to the South Pole.

"There you are!" Aunt Star exclaimed as she popped up off the couch, where she and Aunt Mary had been sitting. They were waiting on her.

"You were expecting me? How long has this been planned?"

"Since last night when Anthony called," Aunt Mary answered.

"Did he tell you I didn't want to do it?"

"He did," Aunt Star said simply. "Noel, we're not here to make you. We'll train you, but the decision you make ultimately must be your own."

"I told your dad that too," Aunt Mary added.

"Fair enough," Noel said with a shrug. "Where is everyone?"

"I left Blaine and Kris at home," Aunt Mary answered.

"Declan is at work, and the kids are at school," Aunt Star answered.

"Will it be just the three of us like this most days?" Noel asked.

"It will during the week, at least until the kids get home from school. Why don't you get settled, and we'll start tomorrow?" Aunt Star suggested.


"I can't believe you're going to be living here in the South Pole!" Angel squealed when she got home from school to find Noel there.

"Me either." Noel did not share Angel's enthusiasm.

"How long will you be here?"

"I don't know. No one can tell me anything, except that I have to do this."

"I know it's not what you want to do with the rest of your life, but it will be so awesome to have you here."

Sure, maybe that was the silver lining that Mom was so desperate to find.

"I wish Gloria could be here too."

"Why would she need to come to the South Pole to train when she could get real world training?"

"Do you think Mom and Aunt Mary will take you on actual hunts, like a field trip?"

"This isn't school. It's assassin training."

"Assassin training? Oh, that sounds cool. I wonder if it will impress boys or scare them?"

"Angel, can you hear yourself? I'm not doing this to pick up guys. I didn't even choose to do this. It's some kind of punishment or something."

"Punishment for what? You don't think Mom and Aunt Mary will be that hard on you, do you? Oh, if that's the case, they should have gotten Mrs. Vivienne. I've seen her when she fusses at those three boys of hers, and she is terrifying."

"She probably has to be. She's the only girl in the house."

"I know. Can you imagine? So, what did they teach you today?"

"Nothing. We're going to start tomorrow."

"Oh, ok. I'm sure it won't be that bad. Mom and Aunt Mary wouldn't actually hurt you or anything."

"Angel, homework," Aunt Star prompted with a cheerful voice.

They didn't talk much more that night on account of Angel's homework and strict school night bed times.

Aunt Mary was staying with Vivienne while she was there for training purposes. Noel was to stay in Angel's room, but she wasn't held to as strict a bed time as long as she didn't disturb Angel.

The next day was torture as far as Noel could tell. The day started with an early morning to get the others to school on time. Noel stayed at the house while Aunt Star took the others to school. Aunt Mary got there not long before Aunt Star got back.

"So, I guess there's no time like the present. You ready to get started?" Aunt Star's question was directed at both Noel and Aunt Mary, but they both appeared to be waiting on Noel's answer.

"We might as well," Noel answered without enthusiasm.

"Right, so what do you know about vampires?"

"I don't know. I know dad was a vampire."

"What else?"

"They drink blood." Aunt Mary and Aunt Star were staring at Noel waiting patiently for more information. "They have demonic powers."

"Do you know what kind of powers?" Aunt Mary quizzed.

"No."

"That's ok. We'll talk about that," Aunt Star assured her.

"What else can you tell us?" Aunt Mary continued.

"That's it," Noel shrugged.

"For a vampire, your dad sure didn't teach you much," Aunt Star commented.

"I'm not surprised," Aunt Mary said. "That wasn't a very pleasant time in Anthony's life. It's not something he likes talking about. It is probably the last thing he wants to talk to his children about."

"Ok, well, I think we should start with a conversation about vampires," Aunt Star suggested and led Noel and Aunt Mary into the living room to sit down comfortably.

Once they were all seated, Aunt Mary asked Aunt Star, "Where do you want to start?"

"Let's start in the beginning," Aunt Star responded. "No one is really sure about how vampires got their start. Did the devil possess a willing volunteer or an unknowing victim? We know today that the possession can be passed from one vessel to another, and taking Anthony's case into consideration, all are not willing volunteers."

"That may or may not be the case in most cases. Regardless, it is a demon possession, and should be taken very seriously," Aunt Mary added.

"A demon possession, Aunt Mary? Really?"

"Yes, really!" Aunt Mary narrowed her eyes at Noel. "You said yourself that vampires possess demonic powers. How could any said person possess demonic powers without a demon possessing said person?"

Noel hated to admit, "I don't know," but she hated even more the idea that her dad was ever possessed by a demon.

"It's not a pretty fact, but it is what it is," Aunt Star said sympathetically.

"What does that make our magic then? Angelic possession?" Noel dared.

"Of course not, our magic is a God given talent."

"Ok, so you think vampires are demon possessed. What next?" Noel asked trying to push forward.

"No, Noel. We know that vampires are demon possessed. I think the first case was a willing volunteer who then sacrificed others' will. I think that each one the first case turned then turned others, and thus the vampire population grew over time to what we know today. I even think that the first case could have been an entire cult rather than just one, but I know they are demon possessed," Aunt Mary said hotly.

"Ease up, Mary. She didn't mean any harm. She just honestly doesn't know any better," Aunt Star scolded. Then she looked to Noel and with a tender tone said, "Baby, none of us like it any more than you do, but unfortunately, the demon possession isn't under question. You'll see that for yourself someday."

"I just don't believe the same way you and Aunt Mary do," Noel protested.

"I know you think you don't, honey, but this isn't a question of whether or not you think it's fair."

"I didn't say it was unfair. I said I don't agree. Now that you mention it, though, it isn't fair. What did people like my dad ever do to you?" Noel didn't wait to hear their answer. She grabbed a jacket and went outside. Walking around the house, she found a spot out of sight and sat down in the snow her back resting against the house.

Her dad was not demon possessed. How could Aunt Star and Aunt Mary say those things? Especially Aunt Mary, she was so cold about it. Tears swelled up in Noel's eyes. Realizing that opened the flood gates, and tears rushed down her face in a loud, breathless, messy sob. She cried until her eyes had nothing left to cry.

She leaned her head back against the house and thought about how badly she wanted to go home. She wished Mom were there. She wouldn't have let them say those horrible things about Dad.

Noel didn't notice Aunt Mary until she sat down next to Noel and pulled an electric blanket over the both of them. The blanket was powered by magic. Noel had not noticed how cold she was getting until she felt the welcome heat of the blanket.

"There's something I want to tell you," Aunt Mary said somberly. "I want to tell you how I came to know your dad. I knew him long before he married your mom. I knew him before your mom was born.

"Once upon a time, I was engaged. Not to Blaine, but to a man who lived long before Blaine. His name was Timothy. I loved him so much… One night, he was viciously attacked by a coven of vampires who brutalized his body, and drained him of all blood. I wasn't there… He had stepped outside for just a minute, and I was headed to join him… I was too late. So many vampires hovered over Timothy's dead body feasting on his blood. I stared into Anthony's eyes that night as I memorized the face of every vampire there, and I vowed to avenge Timothy's death.

"Anthony was there with Timothy's blood dripping down his chin. All I could see that night were monsters who had killed the man I loved, and all I could feel was hate. I hated them for slaying the love of my life, and I hated myself for not being there for Timothy when he needed me most.

"I spent the next two hundred years chasing down every vampire responsible, and I killed everyone except Anthony. I never got to Anthony Phillips, because God had other plans for his life. Anthony Clause is off limits, but I was tempted. I hated him. I hated myself, and he hated himself. It took a long time for the two of us to forgive and move on, and we never would have been able to do it on our own.

"I found out later that Anthony was not technically involved in the killing. His coven killed Timothy. He was already dead when Anthony succumbed to the over powering thirst, but that is not the point. The point is that your dad did horrible, terrible things in his lifetime. There was thirst and urges that he fought, but in the end, he lost the battle each time. He went to the South Pole in an attempt to remove himself from temptation at the very real threat of starvation.

"I understand why your dad didn't want to discuss this with you before, but you need to understand that he was demon possessed. It wasn't a life he chose, but the demon chose him. I'm not saying it is fair. That's just the way it is. Your dad was blessed to be saved by the grace of God."

"You never wanted to be a vampire hunter?" Noel asked.

"I didn't when I was your age, no."

"Why do you really do it? Aunt Star quit when she married Uncle Declan. Why didn't you quit when you married Uncle Blaine? Why do you still do it?"

"I do it, because Timothy died. That was my catalyst moment. That night I was filled with a drive to eradicate demon possession." Aunt Mary sighed and continued, "For me there was no choice. I know you think your parents are being unfair about this, but they are being lenient compared to the way my dad reacted to my reluctance. He didn't talk me into it. He meant I was going to do it, and there was no discussion about it. I'm glad he did."

Noel looked at Aunt Mary like she might be insane.

"I didn't like it at the time, but it was what God wanted. This is my calling. It took Timothy's death to give me a passion for it, but I have no doubt that I am doing what God called me to do. In the same way, I am sure your dad was turned for a reason. The things we go through make us who we are, and God had big plans for your dad's life. He has big plans for your life too."

"How do you know?"

"Because you're here. God wouldn't have put you on this earth if he didn't have a plan for your life."

They must have been out there for a while, because Noel heard Aunt Star and the other kids walking inside the house where they had just gotten home from school.

"Noel... there are two things that I want you to take away from our talk. A, make no mistake about it; vampires are demon possessed. B, vampire hunting is a calling. You may or may not feel a passion for it right away, but if you are sure that it is not your calling, if you feel God calling you in a different direction, you need to follow God's will... I want you to do something for me. Pray. Star and I agreed to train you, and we will. As we train, though, I need you to pray constantly about the training and God's calling for your future. When we're finished, I want you to be able to tell your parents with confidence that vampire hunting either is or is not your calling."

"It's not what Dad wants to hear."

"I know it feels that way now. He has his own sort of passion for the job because of his personal history, but when it comes down to it, all he really wants is for you to follow God's will for your life."

"I don't think so. He thinks there won't be enough hunters if all the available Clauses don't take up arms or something like that."

"Your dad worries too much. God will provide, and Anthony will remember that. Calder is already determined to take up arms as you put it. I don't think Vivienne's other boys are far behind him either. Sometimes it takes an early calling to allow time for training. They're not Clauses though, are they?"

"No."

"Things are changing. The North Pole and South Pole are slowly coming back together. The Clauses have been doing things on our own for a long time now. We are set in our ways. It's just going to take us a little time to fully accept that we are not alone anymore."

Noel had a lot to think about, a lot to pray about.

Chapter Twelve

The next morning Noel woke up to the smell of bacon and freshly baked sugar cookies. The whole house was filled with the aroma of the strange combination. That would turn out to be the best part of the day. The rest of the day was long and boring as Aunt Star and Aunt Mary went over how to spot a vampire.

"Most vampires prefer dark, but that doesn't mean that you'll never see one during the daylight. That myth about them being light sensitive is some nonsense the humans came up with. It's not even logical if you think about it. Sunlight gives off heat. Demons come straight from the depths of hell, so why would a little heat bother them?" Aunt Star was babbling.

"Star, you're getting off point," Aunt Mary scolded. "You can find vampires any time of the day or night. They have no restrictions as far as that goes, but you can't work twenty-four seven."

"How are you supposed to know when to hunt them?" Noel challenged.

"That's entirely up to you," Aunt Star answered.

"You can do some recon and determine when is the most active time for the area you're in, or you can simply pick the hours when you feel you are most at the top of your game," Aunt Mary elaborated.

"What do the two of you do?"

"I work nights most of the time, because what I've found to be true is that they are more active at night," Aunt Mary answered.

"I worked mornings right after my daily bacon and sugar cookie. I was always energized after I had my favorite meal," Aunt Star recalled.

"Her and Vivienne both are morning people," Aunt Mary scowled. Aunt Mary was definitely not a morning person. "Israel works mornings as well, and North chose more of an eight to four schedule so that he could spend more time with his family as the kids were growing up."

"Does he still work during the day like that now that his kids are grown?"

"Yeah, once you create a pattern or a routine, you've acquired more of a specialty. It is best to continue what you know," Aunt Star provided.

"A specialty? Why does it matter what time of the day you hunt them?"

"For the same reason, I can't stand Star and Vivienne's bubbliness first thing in the morning. We have different personalities. So do vampires. You're going to find they are not all the same. They'll react different to different situations, and different reaction times, and place importance on different things," Aunt Mary explained.

"That's right. That's why Joseph hunts at night. He is more of a night life party animal. You'll find that doesn't change in vampires. If they were party animals before the possession, they tend not to give that up," Aunt Star added.

"Did either of you ever hear from Uncle Joseph?" Noel inquired.

"I talked to him. Things are complicated he said, but he is absolutely fine," Aunt Mary reported.

"But, who was that girl with him?"

"A friend."

Aunt Mary and Aunt Star shared a conspiratorial look and said together, "Or more."

"Enough of Joseph's personal life. We're supposed to be talking about vampires," Aunt Star redirected.

"Won't the vampires stand out in a crowd?" Noel questioned.

"Not at all," Aunt Mary answered simply.

"They have no visibly distinguishing marks. They look exactly as they had before the possession. Nothing changes in their appearance," Aunt Star continued.

"Then how do you know they are a vampire? Couldn't they just be one very odd person? What if you kill an innocent person?"

"You won't," Aunt Star assured her.

"You'll learn to use your magic to feel for a demonic presence. There is really no good way to teach that, but you pick it up as you go. Until then, you investigate. Keep your eyes peeled. If you see someone acting suspicious or unethical, keep a close eye on them. None of us are perfect, so they could be an unaffected human. That's why you watch. You don't want to act rashly and kill a human," Aunt Mary expounded.

"But, how do you know? What are you watching for?"

"It's hard in the beginning. It's not easy to accept, but you won't be able to save everyone. When you are first starting out, you're basically waiting to see them sink their teeth into someone. Sometimes you'll intervene in time, and sometimes you won't," Aunt Star described.

"Then what's the point? You didn't save the victim," Noel protested.

"No, you didn't, and those faces will haunt you. The truth is vampire hunting is a learning process just like anything else. You have to keep telling yourself that even though you didn't save this one, by killing just one vampire, you saved hundreds, thousands, or even more."

"It is a war," Aunt Mary said quietly, so quietly Noel almost didn't hear her. "Every war has casualties. It was never meant to be easy. War never is, and the devil is most assuredly waging war. Timothy was a casualty of war that I will never forget. There have been more. There are faces all throughout my career that I will always remember. That's good. To forget would mean you're becoming desensitized to all the bloodshed. If that happens, you'll become cold or calloused or just lose sight of why you're doing what you're doing."

"For the first month, I called North every day and cried," Aunt Star admitted.

"I never knew that," Aunt Mary said.

"North is good at keeping secrets. I was so sure of myself when I left home. I was striking out to change the world, and I wouldn't stop until every last vampire was gone."

"What happened?" Noel inquired.

"The real world happened. I underestimated how hard it would be. I underestimated how many vampires there were in the world, and I overestimated my own preparedness. The truth is no matter how prepared you are, it's not easy."

"Is that why you quit?"

"Me? No, no, I learned to move past it. The pain, the horror, the inadequateness. Finally, I learned to see that I was making a difference. That was what I had really wanted all along. I wanted to know that my contribution mattered, and it did. I quit to take my place at Declan's side. If he ever decided to leave the South Pole for any reason, I would pick up right where I left off."

"Would you really?"

"Sure, if God wants me to fight again, he will provide the way. The same is true for you. If He wants you to fight, he will put you in that situation."

"You make it sound so simple."

Aunt Star chuckled and said, "When dealing with demons, nothing is simple."

For the rest of the afternoon they went over characteristics of vampiric activity, what to watch for, how to investigate without being caught, and when it was best to intervene.

Learning about vampiric powers was more than disgusting. That was more than she had ever wanted to know about her Dad's past. Noel didn't want to think about Dad seducing anyone, even Mom. No

matter how he did it, with magic or not, it was none of Noel's business. Still knowing a demon's strengths was important to protecting yourself. According to Aunt Mary, what you don't know about an opponent will always hurt you.

Noel had thought when she came to the South Pole that her training would consist of physical violence. She didn't realize there would be so much academia to learn.

Aunt Star had not been gone long to pick the kids up from school when Noel asked if she could go visit Princess.

"That's the bear cub you found?" Aunt Mary wanted clarification.

"Yes."

"Your mom knows, right? And, she's ok with it?"

"Sure. I grew up with a full grown polar. Why wouldn't she be ok with it?"

"I had to check. Be back before dark. I'm about to head back to Vivienne's, but I'll let Star know where you are."

"Thank you. Love you, Aunt Mary."

"Love you too, precious."

Noel was on her way to the den when she spotted Princess. She was running about on the ice, clearly playing. It broke Noel's heart to see Princess playing all alone, so she broke stride and started for where Princess was playing.

Without warning Princess pushed off the ice and through a hole into the water.

"Princess!" Noel called desperately as she took off in a fast run. She had every intention of going after Princess, but a strong arm banded across her middle and lifted her right off the ice.

"What are you doing, Clause?"

Kellen. He sounded agitated too.

"I have to get to Princess! Let me go!" Noel kicked and thrashed wildly in attempt to get away from Kellen.

"Hey, shh, calm down. She's alright." Kellen was using soft, calm tones speaking right next to Noel's ear.

"She can't swim!"

"Sure. she can. She's a polar bear. It's instinctual."

"Put me down!"

"So, you can do what? Jump in? She has natural insulation. You'll freeze to death."

"I have to help her."

"She doesn't need your help. Quit fighting me. Look here she comes."

Princess hopped up on top of the ice and shook the excess water from her fur. Finally, Kellen released Noel, and she ran as fast as she could to Princess. The second Princess spotted Noel, she trotted happily toward Noel. Noel fell to her knees and hugged Princess close. "What were you doing? You scared me to death. Don't you ever do that again."

"Clause... She's a polar bear. You're scolding her for doing what all polar bears do. She was just being a polar," Kellen pointed out, but there was no room in Noel's world right now for rational thoughts.

"What are you doing here anyway?"

"I'm here to feed her before hockey practice. I'm the one who lives in the South Pole, remember? What are you doing here?"

"I'm here to train with my aunts."

"Train for what?"

"I'd rather not talk about it," Noel said pushing to her feet. "Come on, Princess. Let's get back to the den so that you can eat."

Without a word, Kellen gathered bottles off the ice where he had obviously dropped them in haste. Noel started walking away assuming that he would follow.

"You're all wet," Kellen told Noel when they got back to the den.

Noel looked down and realized that her clothes were indeed wet where she had been holding Princess. "Yeah," Noel dried her clothes with a nonchalant wave of her hand in front of her chest. "Thanks for stopping me back there. I guess I over reacted."

"You guess? You were about to take an arctic swim. Do you know how long it takes to freeze to death in there?"

"Not really."

"You'll pass out in less than fifteen minutes and die in less than an hour."

"Why do you know that?" Noel wondered.

"It's science. Didn't you ever take science classes?" Kellen returned.

"I took science classes, and I never learned that."

"Maybe you should have. It's just as cold in the North Pole. Maybe you wouldn't have been so eager to dive into freezing waters. What do you learn in the North Pole anyway?"

"I don't know. More practical stuff."

"Right, knowing that jumping into freezing waters would kill you is not at all practical. What is considered practical for Clauses?"

"Never mind, just give me the first bottle."

Kellen passed the first bottle to Noel, who warmed it and fed it to Princess. It didn't occur to her until the bottle was half gone, that Kellen might have taken offence to her waltzing in and taking over feeding Princess. It was his job now after all.

"I'm sorry. I didn't mean to just take over," she apologized. "Do you want the bottle back?"

"No. You don't bother me. Did you warm it?"

"Mm-hmm."

Kellen nodded. "I've been trying to do that, but so far it hasn't worked so well."

Princess took bottle after bottle until every drop had been sucked down. Then she moved to Kellen's lap, snuggled close, and fell right to sleep. Noel watched her wistfully. It was obvious that their relationship had been growing since she had been gone.

"She likes you," Noel commented.

"Yeah, I guess she does. I'm going to have to leave for practice in a little while. Can I walk you back to town?"

"I think I'm going to stick around here for a while."

Kellen shifted clearly uncomfortable and jostled Princess still asleep in his lap. "I don't know if that's a good idea."

"We're not doing this again are we?"

"I know you have incredible magic, but you nearly jumped into freezing waters."

"I over reacted. I know, but it won't happen again."

"I don't know. I won't be able to focus at practice if I know you're still out here."

"You're not my dad," Noel reminded him hotly.

"I'm not trying to be. I just . . ." Kellen's words trailed off on a sigh.

"I haven't seen her in a while. I've got a lot on my plate right now, and I just wanted to relax with Princess for a few more minutes."

They sat in silence for a minute as Kellen absently scratched behind Princess's ear. "You said you have a full grown polar for a pet in the North Pole, right?"

"Yeah, so?"

"Well, Princess is pretty tame. Maybe you could bring her with you. That way you can still spend time with her, and I won't have to worry about you being out here all alone. Don't girls like sleepovers?" His last remark was a tease.

Noel had to admit, though, it was a good idea. Having Princess around might even take some of the sting out of training. "Alright."

"Good." Kellen began jostling Princess.

"Don't wake her!"

"We've got to go. I can't be late for practice, and no way can I carry her that far. She has to weigh at least a hundred pounds."

"Do we have to?" Noel could hear the whining in her voice, yet she couldn't stop it.

"Yes, she can go back to sleep when you get her home. Princess get up. It's time to go."

Princess popped her cute little head up. "You're going to go home with me," Noel told her.

She pushed up and hopped around the den on all four paws.

"I think she likes that idea," Kellen smiled. His smile was big and luminous. That was the smile that he should always wear. It made him irresistible.

"Yeah, I think she does." Noel liked the idea too. She was super excited to be taking Princess home, adopting Princess. "Come on, Princess. Let's go home."

All Noel's excitement died away, however, when Aunt Star met her at the door with a stunned look. "No. No way. That bear is not coming in my house."

"She's not just any bear. This is Princess."

"Noel, don't get me wrong. I'm glad that you've bonded with a pet of sorts, but Princess just isn't coming in my house. I don't allow inside pets."

Noel just stared at Aunt Star indignantly. Life was so unfair. Her parents were forcing her to come down to the South Pole to train for a future she positively did not want, and now Aunt Star is shooting down the first bit of joy she'd found since coming back down here. There had to be something she could do to convince Aunt Star. It wasn't like Noel was the first Clause to adopt a polar bear. In fact, Mom had done the exact same thing while she was living in the South Pole. The only difference was that Mom didn't have anyone to live with; she was staying in a cave.

Then it happened, Noel's lightbulb moment. "Can I stay in Mom's cave then?"

Aunt Star tilted her head thoughtfully. "It is ok with me, assuming it is ok with your mom."

"Mom won't care. I'm sure she won't. She wasn't much older than I am now when she lived there."

"Ok, but I'm going to call her just to check in."

A minute later, Angel came out. "Is it true? You're leaving?"

"I'm not leaving the South Pole. I'm just going to have my own place. We'll still see each other, especially on weekends."

"Ok," Angel said reluctantly.

"Hey, maybe your mom will even let you sleep over at the cave on weekends!"

"In a cave?" Angel's nose scrunched up at the idea.

"My mom lived there while she was in the South Pole, and even your mom stayed there for a little while. I've seen it once, and it's really cute!"

"Won't it be cold and dirty?"

"No, not at all. It's fully heated just like the houses, and it's all cleaned up and decorated. Mom has all kinds of wildlife photos hanging and some of Noah and his brother."

"Ethan and Noah Nickola?"

"Yeah, Mom and Noah are friends."

"I know, but I thought Ethan Nickola hated all the Clauses."

"Yeah, but him and Mom were friends or something before anybody knew she was a Clause."

"You get really excited about history, almost like Mom, but Mom can go on for hours when she gets started."

"Just trust me the cave is totally livable."

"Well, maybe, but I want to see for myself before I agree to sleep over."

"Deal."

## Chapter Thirteen

Mom was fine with Noel living in her old cave of course, and Noel was moved in only hours later. The cave wasn't spacious by any stretch of the imagination. Noel imagined that it was a rather snug fit with Roscoe. Princess wasn't anywhere near that big yet. Being female, she would never be quite as large as Roscoe, but Princess still had another couple years before she was full grown.

The cave looked like Mom's style. Guess her style hadn't changed much over the years. Noel looked around at the pictures hanging on the walls. There were some amazing shots of wildlife. Mom had a real talent for photography. There were some insanely cool shots of Noah with some of the wildlife. There were even a few shots of Noah and Noel assumed his brother. Noel had never seen him, but that had to be Ethan Nickola. Kellen was the spitting image of his dad. His hair was just a shade darker than his dad's, but that was it. They even had the same skin tone. Where did they get that tan from? I mean, seriously, who manages a tan in the extreme cold? He smiled like his dad too. It was a shame, but Noel had to admit that Ethan Nicola had an extremely nice smile.

Noel snuggled deep underneath the covers and was just about to cut out the lights when Princess bounded up onto the bed. With an amused giggle, Noel moved over and made room for Princess to sleep next to her.

The following morning, Noel woke up to the sounds of Princess's whimpering. "What's wrong, Princess?"

Princess wined again, and Noel heard, "Princess," called somewhere in the near distance. Oh no! No one told Kellen that Noel was moving out here with Princess. How could they? It would have been nearly impossible to get a message past his dad. Kellen must have come out to feed Princess.

Noel jumped out of bed and ran towards the sound of Kellen's nearing voice.

"Clause," Kellen moaned. "What is with you? One day you nearly jump into freezing waters. The next day you're running around in pajamas and no shoes.

Noel looked down at her feet and the cold finally hit her with a vengeance. "Cold, cold, cold," she chanted hopping from foot to foot. "Follow me." Noel ran back to the cave as quickly as she could. She didn't look back, but she could hear Kellen and Princess close on her heels.

She leaped into bed and wrapped her feet in the blankets as Princess trotted inside followed by an awestruck Kellen. "What is this place?"

"This is my place for now, but it was originally my mother's."

"So this is like the cave?"

"The cave?"

"Wow, I can't believe it's still here. Why are there pictures of my dad in here?"

"Those are all pictures my mother took."

"They look professional."

"She's good. You look exactly like your dad. You know that?"

Kellen gave Noel a quelling look. He sat down on the foot of the bed, and Princess jumped up beside him. "Oh here," he said handing the bottles off to Noel. "You're living here now?"

"Yeah, Aunt Star didn't want Princess living inside the house, so I moved out here."

"What's up with all the pictures of my dad?"

"I think my mom and your dad were friends once upon a time."

"Yeah, so Uncle Noah says, but why would your mom keep all these pictures after the way my dad treated her?"

"I don't know. I don't know how your dad treated her, not really. My mom doesn't talk about him much."

"My dad doesn't talk about your mom much either," Kellen admitted. "Uncle Noah does though, and he was willing to tell me the story as long as I didn't tell my dad I knew."

"Really? I know bits and pieces, but I don't think anyone has ever told me the whole story. They definitely don't tell me about what your dad did."

"Why not?"

"I think it's hard for my mom. You can literally see the pain on her face whenever your dad's name is mentioned."

Kellen nodded. "That makes sense. How much do you know?"

"I know that my mom ran away when she was twenty-one and came here. I know that was when she met Noah and Ethan. Then Gam came looking for her. Gam says she shot a fireball at the crowd, but she never meant to hurt anyone. All she was trying to do was flush my mom out. There was also some kind of big show down between the North and South when I was a baby."

"Yeah, Uncle Noah and some others fought with your family. Dad still hasn't forgiven him for that, I don't think. He still calls Uncle Noah a traitor every so often."

"That's terrible."

"Yep."

"Shepherd gets on my nerves sometimes, but I can't imagine pushing him away totally."

Kellen arched an eyebrow in question.

"You remember my brother, Shepherd."

Kellen nodded his understanding. "Dad hasn't pushed Uncle Noah away. They just aren't very close. For the most part, no one ever talks about the past with Dad... That fireball your grandmother threw must have been awesome! People still talk about how huge and terrifying it was."

"Gam is pretty awesome."

"I would love to meet her and your granddad. I think it is so cool what your family does."

"You sound like my dad. Mom says he has always been like a wide-eyed child at Christmas time. What do people down here do for Christmas," Noel asked.

Kellen gave a lazy shrug and said, "We spend Christmas with family. We exchange gifts. There's no talk of Santa or any other Clause; that's for sure. Mostly we do what anyone else would do for Christmas. We remember that Jesus was sent to Earth as a baby."

Noel nodded. "Santa is not that big a deal on Christmas Day in the North Pole either." Kellen looked at Noel like her nose had just grown four feet, so she continued. "Most of the Santa emphasis is on preparation and Christmas Eve. Dad and Papa would never want to take the spotlight from Jesus on

Christmas day. You know? Plus, we don't have the novelty of an unknown Santa leaving gifts like the humans do. He's always just been Dad to us."

"Do you get to help out?" Kellen sounded genuinely interested and even more like Dad.

"Yeah, everyone helps out. It's a huge operation."

"What do you do?"

"I'm in charge of the reindeer."

"That explains a lot."

"What is that supposed to mean?"

"You were drawn to Princess right away. You're an animal freak like Uncle Noah."

"Gee thanks."

"I didn't mean it badly. It was a compliment... Are you ok with her if I take off?" Kellen asked giving Princess a pointed look.

"Yeah, sure."

"Ok, I'm going to split. I've got to get to school, and I'm running a little behind. I'll tell you our parents' story that Uncle Noah told me sometime."

"Ok."

Kellen stood to leave but looked back at the last second. "Oh, hey, are you going to be around for a while, to take over feeding Princess I mean?"

"Yes, I'll take care of her. Thank you for taking such good care of her, and thank you for saving me from myself yesterday."

"My pleasure, Clause," Kellen chuckled as he left.

"What are we doing this for?" Noel asked her aunts. She was doubled over at the waist. Sweat was pooled up across her face. She was too tired to wipe it away, and so it dripped, causing a puddle in the floor.

"You're soft," Aunt Mary accused.

"What is that supposed to mean? I'm not out of shape."

"For a vet, you're in good shape. For a vampire hunter, you wouldn't last one week."

Noel looked to Aunt Star for help; instead, all she got was a shrug.

"We've been at it for hours. Can we at least take a break?"

"Do you think the vampires will take a break once you get winded?"

"Here you go," Aunt Star chirped handing Noel a pair of shoes. They were pink and blue. Actually, they were pretty cute, but why shoes?

"What are these for?"

"They're cleats for running on the ice," Aunt Star smiled like she had just handed Noel the world.

"Running on ice?" Noel questioned.

"Yep. The best advice you'll ever get is when outnumbered, overwhelmed, or just outmatched, run."

"That advice has kept me alive for centuries," Aunt Mary admitted.

Aunt Star nodded solemnly. "You've got to learn to run flat out for miles even when you're tired, especially when you're tired."

"Put them on, let's go," Aunt Mary ordered. When had Aunt Mary become such a slave driver?

"I can't. I can't," Noel panted.

"Then you're dead."

"What?"

"That's right," Aunt Star backed her sister.

"When you are tired and outnumbered, if you can't run you die. Real life application for today's lesson, you die."

"Today's lesson? What lesson? I haven't learned anything today!" Noel exasperated.

"Yes, you have," Aunt Star smiled. "Today you learned that you are terribly out of shape for a vampire hunter. You'll have to put yourself on a strict exercise regimen."

"One like today?"

"Oh no, one on top of today. If you don't have the discipline for it, we could put you to work with Declan."

Noel gave her aunts an indignant look. "You're both maniacs who are going to kill me. What do you want me to do?"

"How far can you run?"

"I don't know."

"Start her at two miles and go from there?" Aunt Mary suggested looking at Aunt Star.

"She has a long way to go, doesn't she?"

"Declan is more used to amateurs than we are. Maybe sending her to workout with your husband wasn't a bad idea."

"It would work in theory. On the other hand, Declan was really taken with her hockey skills a couple weeks ago. I'm almost afraid he'd take it easy on her in exchange for a little hockey time."

"I don't know that hockey drills would do her much good out on the streets."

"True, we've got to get her in shape fast."

"We'll just have to do it ourselves," Aunt Mary sighed.

Noel couldn't stand the way they were talking about her like she wasn't there, but she liked it even less when they turned their attention back to her.

"Alright," Aunt Star started, "we'll start with two miles. We'll do two miles today then let you off the hook, but tomorrow morning you'll be expected to get up early and do another two miles before coming over here."

"Running?" Noel asked in disbelief.

"Yes, running. Now put the shoes on, and let's go," Aunt Mary barked.

## Chapter Fourteen

By the time they got back from their two-mile run, Aunt Mary and Aunt Star were barely winded. Noel could barely breath, and moving? Forget about it. She used magic to get back to the cave, because there was no way she could have made that trek.

Thankful that she had thought to stock the fridge the day before, Noel nearly emptied it again feeding Princess. She did good with solid foods, yet she still needed the nutrients she got from the milk. Noel felt bad about it, but she just couldn't move enough to mix bottles. She'd feed Princess extra milk in the morning.

With that thought, Noel collapsed onto the bed and was asleep by the time her head hit the pillow.

The next morning, she hurt from head to toe. The last thing she wanted to do was return to Aunt Star and Aunt Mary, the slave drivers. She didn't much want to run two miles before returning to them either. She had given her word that she would train. She felt foolish, though, putting herself through so much torture for a life she would never choose.

Somehow Noel managed to roll herself out of bed and mix up bottles for Princess, who sucked at the bottles like she was starving. Poor baby, she probably wasn't sure when her next meal would be. Noel vowed to do better no matter how much her aunts put her through, she wouldn't neglect Princess like that again.

Reluctantly Noel dressed and forced herself out into the cold for her daily dose of running. Strangely enough, the more she moved the better she felt. She was soaked with sweat and in desperate need of a shower, but she didn't want to give herself time to stiffen again. So, using magic she transported to Aunt Star's living room.

Of course, both of her aunts were waiting on her as usual. No matter how good Noel thought she was doing or how early she thought she was, her aunts were always one step ahead of her.

"So, what's today's punishment?"

"Kick boxing," Aunt Star said with her bubbly disposition.

"Kick boxing?"

"Exactly, a workout and self-defense in one," Aunt Mary responded. "Any time you can, always try to kill two birds with one stone. That's not necessarily a part of your training. It's just good advice for life."

"Absolutely true," Aunt Star agreed.

"I had Calder doing this last night, and he loved it. Try to have fun with it."

"You mean you went back to Vivienne's last night and did more exercising?" Noel spluttered.

"Sure, I agreed to show Calder a little while I was here."

With a giggle, Aunt Star told, "He asked me just last week if I could teach him to fight without glitter. That kid has a serious drive to hunt. I don't think I can remember anyone with that kind of drive, not even Joseph."

"Good, so let him take my place," Noel suggested.

"Nice try, kid, but he won't be old enough for another six years. Not to mention, you told your dad

you'd train then talk about hunting again afterwards,"
Aunt Mary reminded.

"He didn't give me much of a choice."

"That's a parent's prerogative. We only want what's
best for our kids," Aunt Star said.

"Or, in my dad's case, what he thinks is best for
the world."

"The man has a big heart."

The kickboxing went on for hours, and when they
were done, they ran again. Another two miles. It really
wasn't fair. What had Noel ever done to them to make
them hate her so much? When she finally left it was
with more instructions for the next day. Unbelievably,
Aunt Mary had upped Noel's running distance to two
and a half miles. She had barely made it through the
final two they had done that day, and now she was
supposed to run further?

It wasn't easy, but upon returning to the cave,
Noel forced herself to mix up milk for Princess and
feed her. Noel fell asleep with the last bottle still in
hand. She woke up the next morning still in a sitting
position, the bottle clutched tight in her fist, and
Princess curled up at her side fast asleep.

The next day her aunts had Noel hopping everywhere. She did squats and jumped up from the squat. She would do pushups and jump up from the floor. They even had her jumping back and forth over an X taped onto the floor. It was all exhausting, and Noel was beginning to feel ridiculous. What did any of this stuff have to do with fighting?

Finally, the day ended with another two-and-a-half-mile run.

"Tomorrow I want you to run three miles in the morning and three more in the evening. We'll take the weekend off, but you keep the running up. Three miles each time," Aunt Mary instructed.

"Really? We're taking the weekend off?" Noel asked excitedly.

"Yeah, five days a week is good enough," Aunt Star agreed. "Take two days off. Run and relax. We'll hit it again hard next week."

"So, Angel and I can just hang out this weekend?"

"Sure, if you want to hang out at the rink. Angel is trying to earn some extra money for a new iPad. Declan agreed to let her do some odd jobs around the rink."

"Oh, ok."

The next morning, Noel didn't want to move much less get out of bed and go to a hockey rink. This was her day off, and she was going to sleep in. Angel would have to wait; Noel would get there when she got there. She rolled over and snuggled closer to a squirming Princess.

"Clause? You in there?" Kellen's voice called from outside the cave.

Noel groaned and pulled the covers over her head.

"Wow, that will never get old," Kellen said letting himself in. "Are you still in bed?"

"No, it's an optical illusion," Noel smarted back.

"I told Uncle Noah you were staying here. He tried coming by yesterday and the day before. He said that Princess needs to learn to hunt. Without her mother to teach her, Uncle Noah said it's up to us."

"How exactly do you teach a polar bear to hunt? Why can't we just keep feeding her?"

"Are you serious? She'll never survive out here if she can't fend for herself."

"Roscoe survives just fine."

"That's your pet polar in the North Pole, right?"

"Mmm."

"How many other polars does he have to compete with in the North Pole?" He was right, of course. There weren't any wild animals in the North Pole. Besides Roscoe, the reindeer were the only other animals in the North Pole.

"Alright, smarty pants, what would you suggest?"

"We teach her to hunt."

"What is with the we stuff?"

"I'm going to be around to help. It sounds like I can be around more than you. Why are you still in bed?"

"I can't move," Noel whined pathetically.

"Why?"

"My aunts are working me too hard. They expect me to run three miles this morning, tonight, and the same routine tomorrow on my days off."

"Three miles isn't that bad. I run five miles every day."

"Why?"

"To stay in shape for hockey."

"Huh."

"Come on. Get up. If you have any bottles, I'll start feeding Princess while you get dressed. When she's done I'll run with you."

"There's some in the fridge I mixed last night."

Princess bounded off the bed at the mention of food. Then Kellen took her outside to feed her, leaving Noel some privacy to get dressed. Noel pushed herself out of bed and shrugged into loose-fitting sweats. She seriously did not want to be getting ready to run, but she did want to spend a little time with Angel. The sooner she got the run out of the way the sooner she could hang out with Angel.

Princess gulped down the milk, and they were ready to go. Kellen was in way too good a mood for someone about to run three miles.

"This will get me warmed up for my hockey lesson today."

"Lesson, not practice?"

"I'm working with Coach Declan today."

"Me too. Well, I mean not me. Angel is working for Uncle Declan to make some extra money, so I'm going to hang out there."

"Oh yeah, she's Coach Declan's daughter, right? How old is she?"

"Almost fifteen. How old are you?" Noel shot back. Kellen had sort of put her on the defense asking about Angel's age. What business was it of his how old Angel was?

"Nineteen."

"Nineteen? I thought you were still in school."

"Yeah, so? I have a late birthday. My parents held me back a year to give me time to mature. How old are you?"

"Eighteen."

"Shouldn't you still be in school?"

"You can move at your own pace when you're homeschooled. I finished last year."

"You're pretty smart then?"

"There just wasn't much to do in the North Pole but work and school."

"Oh, I'm sorry. What time are you going to the rink?"

"I don't know. After we finish the run I guess."

"I'll walk you there," Kellen offered.

"I don't need an escort."

"I know, but I'm going to the same place. Why wouldn't we walk together?"

"You could have started with that," Noel accused.

"I said I was working with Coach Declan today. Where did you think I was going?"

"You didn't say what time today."

Princess, who had been keeping pace with Noel and Kellen, rushed ahead and leapt head first into a snow drift. Snow went flying in every direction as she kicked franticly.

"Princess is in a good mood," Kellen commented.

"Yeah, she is."

"That's good. She wasn't while you were gone. I played with her and everything, but I think she missed you. It's good that you're back."

Yeah right. It sure didn't feel like a good thing to be back. At least some good was coming of her forced training. She wanted Princess to be happy, and she enjoyed spending time with Angel too.

"So, your aunts have you running every morning?"

"Yes, I have to run before I report to them for torture duty."

"Torture duty?"

"They would call that an exaggeration, but I swear it's not. They're going to kill me."

Kellen gave Noel a perplexed look just before Princess came to a complete halt in front of them and proceeded to shake snow from her fur.

"Princess!" Noel shrieked.

"That was on purpose, bear," Kellen accused then tackled Princess from the side.

He did. He really did. He tackled her, a defenseless baby cub… Maybe not so defenseless. Princess was holding her own pretty well. Actually, she was good at the game, and it was a game, one that they had obviously played many times before.

Noel jogged in place to watch for a minute. She didn't want to stiffen up. She knew she wouldn't be able to move again once she stiffened up, but she wanted to watch Kellen and Princess fighting. Princess might have missed Noel while she was gone, but Noel was betting that Princess wasn't too miserable. She looked perfectly thrilled to be rough housing with Kellen.

After a minute, Noel started her run again leaving Kellen and Princess behind. "Hey, wait up!" Kellen called out as he hurried to catch up. "Take that trail to your right. It will circle us back around to your cave, and it will be right at three miles."

Noel nodded and made the turn.

"It sounds ridiculous talking about returning to your cave, like you're some cave woman or something."

"A cave woman?" Did he seriously just say that? It was somewhat insulting. Noel didn't think that Kellen meant it to be insulting, but it sort of was. She knew she should let it go. She should worry more about when he called her Clause. That was her name though, no matter how much his family didn't like it.

"Yeah, you know before people figured out how to build houses… never mind. What are your aunts training you for anyway?"

"My future."

"You have to get in shape for your future with animals?"

"Who said anything about animals?"

"You did. You said that taking care of the animals was your job at the North Pole."

"It is my job at the North Pole, but I won't always be at the North Pole, will I?"

"Why not? Do you not like it there?"

"I love the North Pole, but tradition says that the oldest male takes over the job of Santa. Other siblings leave the North Pole."

"Oh." Kellen looked like he didn't know what to make of that, and that was just fine by Noel. She was not in the mood to go into any more detail about what her future held or didn't hold.

"So, where do you go?"

"All over."

"So, you could end up down here?"

"What? No."

"Your aunt, Mrs. Star, ended up here," Kellen pointed out.

"Not until almost two and a half centuries later."

"Oh… Where did she live before she came here?"

"Lots of places. I think mostly Hollywood."

"Oh… Where does your other aunt live?"

"Aunt Mary? She lives in New York."

"Oh… Where does the rest of your family live?"

"I think Uncle Joseph spends most of his time in Vegas. He likes to party. At least I think he likes to party. I've never seen it, but that's what everyone says. Uncle North and Uncle Israel move around too much to call any one place home."

"Why do they move around so much?"

"Work."

"Oh."

That was the end of conversation during their run. Kellen got quiet and thoughtful, like he was trying to absorb everything Noel had told him. Noel really didn't think she had told him all that much. Whatever.

As they walked to the ice rink, Kellen told Noel everything Noah had told him about what happened when Ethan attacked the North Pole. It wasn't pleasant either. Ethan had taken a whole group of men to the North Pole then played on Mom's emotions to get through the wards surrounding the North Pole. One of the men actually tried to shoot Papa. It didn't work, but why would anyone want to point a gun at Papa much less pull the trigger?

Ethan was just as bad. He had held a knife at Mom's throat. The idea that Mom still loved him as much as she did was absurd. The guy had tried to kill her, yet she still cared for him deeply. To hear Mom tell it Ethan is as much a brother to her as Noah is. That's saying a lot too.

All's well that ends well, Noel supposed. Papa was alive. Mom was alive. Ethan Nicola still hated the Clauses, but it seemed the old saying was true. You just couldn't have your cake and eat it too. That didn't mean that Noel had to like Kellen's dad.

Chapter Fifteen

"You just walked in here with Kellen Nickola," Angel whispered dramatically, as if Noel didn't know who she had been walking with.

"Yeah, so?"

"So? So, that's hot. That's what so."

Good grief, Noel thought. "It was kind of cold outside. We are in the South Pole."

"Hardy, har, har. You laugh, Noel, but Kellen Nickola is hot."

Noel couldn't argue that fact. The guy really did look good. She turned and watched Kellen lace up his skates. Muscles bunched along his shoulders. His dark hair shined in the florescent lighting. Noel couldn't see his eyes from this distance, yet she knew they were a darker but no less pure a blue than the sky. Noel would love to have a complexion as impossibly dark as Kellen's.

"So, what were you doing with Kellen?" Angel persisted.

"Nothing. He just came by to give me a message from Noah."

"His uncle? Why?"

"It was about Princess. Apparently, Noah had been out to the cave to talk to me, but I wasn't home."

"So, Kellen Nickola came to your house cave thing?"

"Yeah, so?"

"So, be careful. The South Pole isn't that big, and people talk."

"So?"

"So, Kellen's dad will freak out if he finds out Kellen was talking to a Clause much less visiting one."

"It's not like anybody saw us."

"You don't think. People are always watching to pick up on the latest gossip," Angel cautioned.

"Fine, I've been warned. Can we talk about something different now?"

"Sure. What was the message Kellen delivered?"

"I'm going to have to teach Princess to hunt."

"You're kidding, right?" Angel giggled.

"No."

Apparently, that was too funny, because Angel nearly fell in the floor laughing. She was doubled over she was laughing so hard.

"What is so funny?" Noel demanded.

"Mom and Aunt Mary are teaching you to hunt, and you have to teach Princess to hunt."

Ok, that was kind of funny, a little, and even Noel chuckled.

Uncle Declan shot the girls a dirty look, and Angel got back to work on whatever it was she was doing. Noel didn't know much about hockey. She knew even less about running an ice rink, and she had no clue what Angel was doing.

"Is there anything I can do to help?" Noel offered.

"Nah, if I don't do the work, I don't get the cash. At least that's what Dad said was his policy."

"Oh. What should I do?"

"You can just hang out. We can talk while I work."

That sounded nice to Noel, a little down time where all she had to do was relax and talk; unfortunately, it didn't last long.

"Noel, gear up," Uncle Declan called over.

Noel sighed but followed directions. Within a few minutes she was moving stiffly padded up from head to toe.

"I want you to play defense," Uncle Declan instructed.

"Uncle Declan, I don't know how to play hockey."

"What do you kids do in the North Pole to keep out of trouble?"

"We work. I tend to the reindeer, and Shepherd works with the elves in the toy factory. We don't have time to get into trouble."

"Ok, what do you do to have fun?"

"I like working with the reindeer and with Roscoe."

"That huge polar bear? I'll never forget the first photograph I saw of you. You were just a baby about a year old sitting on top of that big old bear's back. Ok, just do whatever it takes to keep Kellen from taking a shot at the goal."

"Ok, I can do that."

"Good girl. I knew you could. Alright, set it up, Nickola."

Kellen skated out to the middle of the ice and threw a puck down on the ice in front of him. Noel skated over and asked, "What do we do?"

"Wait for Coach's whistle. When you hear the whistle blow, it's on," Kellen explained.

The whistle shrieked from somewhere back behind Noel causing her to jump and miss Kellen's first move. He gave the puck a quick, hard jab with his stick. The puck went gliding across the ice, and Kellen started flying after it. He was fast, but Noel was faster.

Noel had spent a lot of quality time in a pair of skates racing with Donner. It gave him a chance to run flat out, and Noel was still in control of where he went. She might never be faster than Angel, but Noel was still faster than most people.

Noel raced past Kellen and skidded to a complete halt in front of him. Kellen tried to throw on the breaks, but it was too late. He ran into Noel with a rough thud. The puck went flying off to Noel's right. She twisted around and skated towards the puck. Kellen was right on her heels. Noel got there first, yet there was nothing she could do once she got there. She didn't have a stick. That wasn't right. She should have a stick. Didn't all the players in a hockey game have a stick?

Noel kicked the puck away, but it didn't take much for Kellen to reach out with his stick and stop the puck's momentum. He tried skating around Noel, but he gave himself away by looking to her left at the last second. Noel lunged to her left and crashed into the hardness of Kellen's chest. She abruptly fell to her butt with an oomph.

Kellen skated past unhampered and sent the puck straight into the goal.

"Great," Uncle Declan called. He skated over to Kellen and started talking to Kellen about something Noel couldn't quite make out while Noel pushed back to her feet.

"Again, Noel. Come on. Get moving."

Noel was suddenly unsure who was doing more work, her or Angel. She skated out to the middle of the ice where Kellen had set up with the puck again.

This time Noel was ready for the high-pitched whistle. It still wasn't too pleasant on the ears, but at least it didn't startle her this time.

Noel kicked at the puck. It went sailing out of sight, and Noel skated into Kellen bumping him in the opposite direction than what she had kicked the puck.

"What are you doing, Clause?" Kellen asked.

"Whatever works," Noel answered as she continued to push.

Kellen started pushing back, maybe a little harder than Noel had expected, because she fell to her butt for a second time. Kellen didn't waste any time. As soon as Noel went down, he was off to the races and sent the puck straight into the goal.

He looped back around and held a hand out to Noel. "What ya' doing down there on the ice, Clause?"

Noel accepted the help but narrowed her eyes at the barb. They set up for a third time and waited for the whistle. Kellen knocked the puck away. The puck went to Noel's right, but Kellen went to her left. Noel hesitated for a split second unsure which one to follow. That split-second hesitation was all Kellen needed to get a head start. Noel went after Kellen, and Kellen went after the puck only a yard in front of Noel. Kellen pulled the stick back and hit the puck hard across the ice. This time the puck hit the goal frame and bounced the other way.

Before Noel knew they were still going, Kellen had eaten up half the distance between the puck and themselves. He swung again, but this time he didn't miss.

Noel huffed loudly and demanded of Uncle Declan, "Why don't I have one of those sticks?"

"Talk to my equipment manager," Uncle Declan laughed.

Angel met Noel out on the ice with a stick. "Are you letting him get past you?" Angel asked.

"No," Noel grumped. She was, however, getting frustrated. Noel didn't like losing, and it wasn't sitting well now either.

Noel went back to the middle, this time armed with a stick. When Uncle Declan's whistle blew, Noel swung the stick at the puck at the same time Kellen did. Noel's stick glanced off of Kellen's and rammed right into the side of his right skate. He went down in a heap of tangled limbs.

Kellen laid on the ice and laughed as Noel gave the puck a good shove away from them. "What's so funny?" she asked Kellen.

"You're supposed to hit the puck, not me."

"Off the ice, Nickola, and try it again," Uncle Declan barked.

Kellen pushed to his feet and went after the puck. Noel took a minute to peek at Uncle Declan. He was never short with Noel. His face was blank, all business but not necessarily mad. Noel wasn't sure what he was thinking.

"You alright, Clause?" Kellen asked skating up behind Noel.

"Yeah, I guess. Does Uncle Declan look mad to you?"

"Nah, you'd know if he were mad. He yells when he's mad."

"Uncle Declan has never yelled at me!" Noel reacted shocked to the core.

"Well, he yells at his players. Get used to it."

"I'm not one of his players," Noel felt the need to point out. She didn't like the idea of her fun-loving uncle yelling at her, not one bit.

"You're definitely not that," Kellen laughed.

It was a good thing that Kellen did look so good. He had a lot to make up for after he opened that big mouth of his.

They went three more rounds before Uncle Declan moved on to work with Kellen on a different skill. Kellen took two out of the three, but Noel managed to block him on the final round.

## Chapter Sixteen

Angel got permission to sleep over with Noel that night on the one condition that they were both on time for church the next morning. Aunt Star also made a point to stress to Noel that she was the adult in charge and to please act like one.

The cave must have met with Angel's approval, because she didn't insist on going back home immediately.

"Wow," Angel gawked looking around the cave. "I've never seen this place for myself. Did you know that Mama stayed here for a while too?"

"Uh, yeah. I told you that. Remember?"

"Oh yeah. It wasn't for very long, just while her and Dad were dating. I asked. They didn't date for very long before they got married. Every time Mom tells the story Dad makes me and Joy promise not to rush into marriage. Although, I don't think it can be considered rushing into marriage when you think about how old Mom was."

"How old was she when they got married?"

"I don't know for sure. Maybe Mom told me and I forgot, but I know she was older than your dad."

"I don't know how old my dad was when your parents got married, but I know that he was two hundred and forty when I was born."

"Were you born before or after my parents got married?"

"I was a year old when your parents met, because it was when Noah came to the North Pole to fight his brother."

"That means that Mom was more than two hundred and forty years old when she married my dad. See what I mean? That can hardly be considered rushing. Can it? It doesn't matter anyway. There's no one around here that I want to marry anyway."

Angel walked around studying each picture hanging on the wall while Noel gave Princess her evening bottles. It was too bad Princess had to learn to hunt for her own food. Noel was going to miss feeding her.

"Your mom took all these pictures?" Angel asked.

"Yeah, it's some of the ones she took while she was living down here. She's got twice as many at home, though, from the same time. She must have taken a million."

"I love your mom's pictures. She's such a great photographer. I wish I could do that. Do you think she'd teach me?"

Noel shrugged. "She might. It's only fair. Your mom is training me. My mom could teach you photography in return."

"Do you think she really would? I might could go up during the summer! A whole summer to spend at the North Pole learning photography would be so awesome!"

"Better ask your mom," Noel warned. Angel was still only fourteen after all. She would be fifteen by this summer, but still...

"It's not Mom I'd have to convince. She's pretty cool with stuff like that. Dad would be the hard one. He says it's harder to let go of his little girls than he thought it would be. Nickolas gets away with so much more than me and Joy ever did, and he's only nine. Is your dad that way with you and Shepherd?"

"Not really. He's never had to let me go until I came down here, though. Training was his idea, so he sort of has to suck it up."

"Yeah, I'm still glad you're here."

"I'm glad to have time to hang out, but I could do without all the workouts," Noel admitted.

"I didn't know that Kellen looked so much like his dad. It's almost like looking at Kellen in all these pictures. Does your mom have pictures of Mr. Nickola at home too?"

"Yeah, a lot, but she keeps them put away. She pulls them out from time to time, but I've never seen them. I didn't know what Ethan looked like until I saw the pictures here."

"That's really sad. That your mom still misses him so much, I mean."

"I think she believes that he will come around. She's never said that, but it's in the way she looks anytime his name comes up."

"I hope he does. I want your mom to be happy, but I have to be honest. He doesn't have anything to do with my family either, because we have Clause blood."

"I don't care if he does or not," Noel said honestly. "He's shallow and filled with hate. I wouldn't want to be friends with him if he had done me the way he did Mom."

"She must have really loved him."

"All it's gotten her is years of pain. It all happened twenty or more years ago. When is she going to give up on him?"

"I don't think you give up on your friends. I wouldn't ever give up on you and Gloria no matter what you did to me."

"That's different. We're family."

"And, we're friends." Angel climbed onto the bed next to Noel and wrapped her arms around Noel in a gentle hug. "I love you. That will never change. It's probably the same way for your mom."

Noel didn't respond. She wasn't sure how to respond. She understood that Ethan was one of Mom's friends. She could even understand that she would always love him, but how long could you hang onto someone who didn't want to change?

"So, spill," Angel instructed leaning back against the headboard. "What's the deal with you and Kellen?"

"There's no deal with me and Kellen."

"I'm not buying that. What were the two of you doing together this morning?"

"I already told you. He was delivering a message for his uncle."

"There's more to it than that."

"He's just been helping out with Princess. That's all."

"Helping out how?"

"Someone had to feed her while I was gone, and Noah was busy."

"Ok, I get that. He fed Princess while you were gone, so what was he doing over here this morning? Noah could have called Mom or Aunt Mary to give you a message. That makes me think that Kellen was coming over here anyway. Why would that be?"

"I don't know. I guess he bonded with Princess while I was gone. Look at her. She's hard to resist."

Angel petted Princess's head where she had fallen asleep in Noel's lap. "Yeah, she is precious, and yet... I think that you protest too much. There is more going on between you and Kellen, Noel Clause, and I will get to the bottom of it."

"There's nothing to get to the bottom of," Noel insisted.

Angel ignored Noel's insistence. "What's he like?"

"Who?"

"Kellen Nickola."

"Why are you asking me? I don't live here."

"No, but you've had more interaction with him than I have. He's not allowed to interact with Clauses remember. I may be an Anderson, but there is no denying my Clause blood. I've seen him around school, and I've heard Dad talk about him. I've never been around him much, so what's he like?"

"I don't know. He's ok, I guess. He took good care of Princess, and he seems to really care about her."

"He's an animal lover? What else?"

"I don't know him that well. I know him through Princess and through hockey."

"That's right. What was it like to play with him. Y'all looked pretty intense out there on the ice."

"I don't like to lose."

"I know that already. You've been the competitive one for as long as I can remember. Is Kellen really competitive too?"

"I don't know. I think he was really trying."

"Well, I know that. If Dad's students don't give him one hundred percent, he throws them out. He said he's not a public service like the South Pole little league. His students pay for lessons, and if they aren't going to take it seriously, there's no sense in wasting time."

"Your dad is serious about hockey, isn't he?"

"I told him last year that he should have played professionally."

"Did he ever think about playing professionally?"

"Nah, he says he likes the easy-going life here in the South Pole. He says that he has Mama and his kids and that he didn't need anything more."

"Uncle Declan is sweet."

"Dad's a goof."

"I like that about him. He's fun."

"Yeah, he is. I like that too. He's not too old to play. He…"

Noel looked over to see Angel fast asleep. She must have been exhausted, going to school all week and working at the rink on Saturday's. It was getting late. Noel was awfully tired herself, but she still had to run.

She slid Princess off her lap and jotted a quick note for Angel in case she woke up while Noel was gone. The air was crisp and cold. It smelt like fresh fallen snow, which had to be about the best smell in all the world. It was a clean, refreshing smell that always reminded Noel of home no matter where she was. She could almost smell the fresh sugar cookies that Mom kept for Dad and his cookie addiction.

The moonlight shimmered off the snow and ice giving a glow bright enough to see by. The ice sparkled like stars in the night. Up in the clear, black sky stars were scattered across the horizon. Everywhere Noel looked the white hills of snow met the blackened skyline. It was a peaceful time to be outdoors. All was quiet. There were no animals out; none would survive the frigid temperatures of the South Pole at night. The only sound was that of Noel's cleats sinking into the ice as her feet hit the ground. Running in cleats was a special skill. Lucky for Noel, it was one she had learned at a young age out running with the reindeer.

Crunch, crunch, crunch, Noel's feet beat out a steady rhythm, and soon her breathing had evened out to match. The harsh bite of cold air stung slightly as it rushed into her lungs, but Noel welcomed the feeling. It was comfortingly familiar. She could almost see Donner running next to her trying to best her, which, of course, he always did.

Noel had only been here a week, and already she missed Roscoe and the reindeer terribly. How could Dad expect her to live anywhere so far from home on a more permanent basis was beyond her.

# Chapter Seventeen

Church the next morning was… awe inspiring. Living in the North Pole, there wasn't much of a church in the more traditional sense of the word. At home it was just her, Shepherd, Mom, Dad, Gam, and Papa, but here in the South Pole, there was a whole congregation. Angel even had her own Sunday School class. Noel had heard Dad and Gam talk about Sunday School classes, but they were the only two in the North Pole with any familiarity with actual Sunday School classes. It had been a long time since either of them were somewhere where they could attend a Sunday School class. Noel had never attended one. When her family visited the South Pole, they tended to go to the service only. This time Noel was going to be in the South Pole for a while, and Angel was expected to attend Sunday School. So, Noel joined Angel's Sunday School class.

The class age was based on grade level, which meant that Noel was technically too old for the class, but no one seemed in a hurry to separate the two cousins. That was fine by Noel. She didn't want to be separated.

Their lesson came from the book of James. It dealt with the issue of quarreling, which was a lesson that both the North and South Poles could have used several generations ago. That was one of the amazing things about the Bible, though; it was not relevant for only a single specific moment in time. It was relevant for everyone all around the world at any time. The trick was you had to be open to what God was trying to tell you.

Noel tried to keep an open mind and an open heart as the Sunday School leader read, "But if ye have bitter envying and strife in your hearts, glory not, and lie not against the truth. This wisdom descended not from above, but is earthly, sensual, devilish. For where envying and strife is, there is confusion and every evil work." (James 3:14-15)

Most recently Noel had been quarrelling with her parents. She thought about how bitter she had been over the decisions they had made for her, more bitter with Dad than Mom. If Noel were being perfectly honest with herself, and she might as well since she couldn't hide anything from God, she had been envious of Shepherd. It wasn't that she wanted the job of Santa, because she didn't. She had never in her wildest dreams ever wished for that job, but she loved her job with the reindeer. Even though Shepherd wasn't staying to work with the reindeer, he was getting to stay in the North Pole. He was staying in the only home they had ever known. No one was rushing him out insisting that he follow some violent tradition. It wasn't fair. Shepherd had been given no more choice than Noel. He was an innocent by standard, but it hadn't mattered much to Noel in all her bitterness.

Where had all Noel's self-righteous anger gotten her? Absolutely nowhere. She was still in the South Pole, and she was still training to be a vampire hunter. All her anger had done was cause strife between her and her family. What did it matter in the end? The end result was still the same.

Noel had been so focused on everything she considered a grave injustice that she had forgotten to pay attention to all her blessings. She had parents who loved her enough to be worried about her future, whether she always agreed with them about her future or not. That wasn't something that everyone had. Noel was lucky to have such a loving family. Even Shepherd had loved and valued her enough to approach her and explain the side that she wasn't seeing in the argument.

Angel was one of Noel's very best friends. Who cared why she was getting to spend extra time with her? She was. They may not be seeing much of each other during the week, but they were going to have every weekend together. That was more time than they had before. They usually had to settle for phone calls to span the long distances between visits. For that, Noel was grateful.

She got to spend time with two of the world's coolest aunts. They are both passionate about vampire hunting, and despite the fact that Noel had not shown a willing attitude or even a kind attitude, they were still willing to share their passion with her. In the long run, whether or not she made vampire hunting her vocation, this was still a chance to learn something new. Maybe she could learn a little about what things were like for Dad before he found Mom.

Noel had her own place in her Mom's cave. It was the first bit of true independence that Noel had ever been graced with. As far as she knew, no one had been uneasy about the move. That showed that her family trusted her to be responsible enough to live on her own. That was a big deal, especially for an eighteen-year-old. In that respect, Noel was really rather flattered. If she continued to act like a petulant child, she would squander her gifted freedom.

Princess waited back at the cave for Noel. Noel was fairly certain that there was no other family or single person worldwide, outside her own family, with a pet polar bear. Now, Noel had been blessed with not only Roscoe but Princess as well. Her newfound freedom in Mom's cave didn't mean loneliness for Noel, because she did have Princess.

Even having the chance to attend an actual church and a real Sunday School class for the duration of her time down here, was a blessing in itself. Noel had so much going for her, but she had been so focused on the bad, that she let bitterness poison her.

Noel decided then and there that when they got back to Aunt Star's house, she would give Dad a call to apologize. She really wanted to talk to her family anyway. She had never been away from them a whole week before, and she missed them.

The sermon that morning was from the book of James too, which Noel thought was an amusing coincidence. The preacher based an entire sermon off James 5:9. It wasn't hard to do. James 5:9 said, "Grudge not one against another, brethren, lest ye be condemned." Holding a grudge was an easy topic to elaborate on to make quite a long morning. Not to mention it too was a lesson that both the North and South Poles could use.

Noel thought and thought about who she might be holding a grudge against. Noel didn't know as many people as most. Outside her family, the only other people she really knew were Noah and Lorelei, and they were as close as family. That wasn't to say someone couldn't hold a grudge against a family member. It was just that Noel didn't think she was.

The sermon must have some sort of relevance in Noel's life, but for the life of her she couldn't see the relevance in that moment. Nevertheless, she'd keep the message in mind until the relevance was revealed. She had no doubt that God would show her the relevance when the time was right.

That afternoon Aunt Mary cooked lunch while Aunt Star and Vivienne peered over her shoulder. Maybe they'd learn something, but Noel doubted it. Uncle Declan, Uncle Blaine, and Kyson were watching some sort of sporting show with Nickolas, who appeared as if in a daze as he watched. Angel was helping Joy with a school project that was due on Monday. Noel borrowed Aunt Star's sat phone and stepped outside into the quiet, chilly afternoon to call home.

Mom answered after the first ring. "Hello?"

"Hey, Mom."

"Hey, baby. How's it going?" Noel could tell by Mom's tone that she was excited to talk to her and relieved to hear from her. It might have been selfish, but that made Noel feel good.

"It's going alright. Aunt Mary and Aunt Star are working me like drill sergeants. They mean business when it comes to physical fitness. They have me running every morning and evening, and on weekdays we work out from the time I get to Aunt Star's until the time she leaves to pick up the kids."

"It's rough, huh?"

"I'm not as sore as I was at first. I'm even starting to like the tranquility of the run, but don't tell Aunt Mary and Aunt Star. They might push me harder if they find out I'm starting to like it. I got to go to Sunday School with Angel today!"

"Oh, that's good! How did that go?"

"It went really well. The lesson was on quarreling. Mom… I don't want us to fight anymore."

"I don't either, Noel."

"I'm sorry I've been so stubborn. I just… I don't know. I still don't want to hunt vampires, but I shouldn't have been so combative and disrespectful."

"I think that's very mature of you."

"How are things at home?" Noel desperately wanted to know.

"Still busy as ever. One of the conveyor belts in the toy factory wore down and left the elves in a tizzy, so that's kept your brother occupied. Papa keeps grumbling about how he's supposed to relax in retirement. Dad has missed you more than he'll admit. He's been walking around all week in a sour mood."

"I miss y'all too. How are the reindeer?"

"I only had time to take them out once this week."

That wasn't good. The reindeer needed the exercise, and Cookie and Captain needed the daily training reinforcements. This was going to mean a major step backwards for them. That wouldn't fair well for Cupid's pending retirement either.

"Comet and Dasher don't seem to be bothered by that of course, but I think Blitzen is mad. Donner is pouting. I think he just misses you. Captain and Cookie are something else altogether. We're not exactly seeing eye to eye right now, but we'll get there."

Mom was probably being too soft. Captain and Cookie need love and affection, but you had to use a firm approach when it came to their training. Noel hated that she wasn't there to do it herself, but training was something she needed to do no matter where the future led her. "Is Dad there?"

"He is. I love you, baby."

"Love you too, Mom."

"Hey, Noel? How are you feeling?" Dad came on the line.

"I'm tired mostly. I'll be as muscled as Roscoe by the time I get home if Aunt Mary has her way. Her and Aunt Star have me working out hard every single day in addition to running in the mornings and evenings."

"Have you learned anything else?"

"Not much. We did some kick boxing workout regiments. They tried to explain how to spot a vampire, but it was more of how you can't spot a vampire."

"What?"

"You know. There's no visible difference in a vampire from anybody else. It's all about surveillance."

"You'll know a vampire when you see one. There's an evil vibe that they all give off."

"No offence, Dad, but have you encountered a vampire since joining the family?"

"No."

"Then how do you know it wasn't a vampire thing. Maybe vampires can sense one another in a way the rest of us can't. Don't you think if there was a vibe to pick up Aunt Mary and Aunt Star would have noticed it by now?"

"Good point. How is everything besides your training going? You're doing well?"

"I am. I like living in Mom's cave. It's my first taste of freedom, and it's pretty cool. Maybe the next time y'all come down this way Mom can bring me some pictures of you guys that I can hang."

"I think that sounds like a good idea. Your mom enjoyed the cave too. I just marveled over the magic it must have taken."

"You could do it."

"Now I could, but I couldn't back then. I remember the first time I saw it thinking that Clause magic was so incredible that there had to be a way to reverse what had been done to me."

"Yeah, we talked some about how vampires' powers work. I didn't need to know that."

"I'm sorry you had to hear that, but that's the harsh reality."

"Dad, what if there is someone else like you out there? What if you get a letter someday asking for help?"

"Well, I don't know that there is anything I could do, but I'd give it everything I had."

"So, you would try?"

"Sure. That's what I wanted more than anything was just for someone to try to help. If it couldn't be done, then it couldn't, but at least I'd know."

"What if they had just drained a human of all blood, you have a stake poised over his heart, and he cries out for help? Would you hold your hand?"

"I don't know. That would be a judgement call."

"What if I call it wrong?"

"You have to trust in God that he will never lead you wrong."

"What if vampire hunting isn't where God is leading me at all? How can I trust my instincts in a judgement call then?"

"We'll talk about that more when you get home."

"Sure, Dad."

"Papa wants to talk to you. I love you, sweetheart."

"Love you too, Dad."

"Hello?"

"Hey, Papa."

"I've missed you something horrible. Are Star and Mary treating you well?"

"Yes, sir."

"Making you sleep in a cave though, aren't they?"

"Papa," Noel laughed.

"The cave isn't that bad. It's actually really nice. Aunt Star lived there before. Did you know that?"

"I think I heard that somewhere."

"Aunt Star checked with Mom too before she let me go."

"Just so long as they are taking care of my granddaughter."

"They are."

"Good. I love you, baby girl."

"I love you too, Papa."

"Hey, precious!" Gam said.

"Hey, Gam."

"Are you enjoying your time with Angel?"

"I really am."

"I thought you might. A girl needs her best friends close, especially when you get to a fork in the road. I just wish Gloria could be with you two girls right now too."

It was uncanny the way Gam could cut straight to the heart of a thing. Gam had wisdom that most could only hope to achieve. Noel wouldn't be surprised if Gam already knew how this whole thing would play out. She wouldn't admit it if she did. Gam always said that a lesson lived is a lesson learned, but a lesson told is a lesson on hold.

"It's nice that you girls have this time, but I still miss having you here. How long do Star and Mary think your training is going to take?"

"They haven't said, but I get the feeling things are moving slow."

"That doesn't matter. You go at whatever pace you need, and we'll all be here when you get done."

"Thank you, Gam."

"That's what grandmothers are for."

That wasn't always the case for everyone, and Noel knew it. She was grateful for the family she had.

"What have you been up to outside training?" Gam asked.

"I'm taking care of Princess. Noah says I'm going to have to teach her to hunt. I'm not sure yet how I'm going to do that."

"You'll figure it out. You've got your mom's knack with animals."

"I got to hang out with Angel yesterday at the ice rink. Well, I was supposed to. She's working for her dad, and I ended up helping in Kellen's lesson."

"Who is Kellen?"

"He's just a boy."

"Ah, is he cute?"

"I guess so, if you like that sort of thing."

"And, what sort of thing might that be?"

"Black hair, blue eyes, tanned skin, nothing special."

"I'd say that a tan in the South Pole is very special. He takes lessons with Declan, so I am assuming he is in good shape too."

"Sure."

"Mm, hmm, anything else going on?"

"Aunt Star let Angel sleep over at the cave last night since it wasn't a school night. I hope she lets her stay every Saturday night. I won't be down here forever, you know."

"Maybe she will. I'll put in a good word for you girls."

"Thank you, Gam!"

"Sure thing, precious. Talk to your brother a minute."

"Hello?" Shepherd was trying to feign indifference, but Noel knew him better than that.

"Hey."

"Kellen is Noah's nephew, right? What are you doing with him?" He sounded aggressive, yet Noel heard it for the protectiveness is was.

"I was helping Uncle Declan out with his hockey lesson again. I was trying to keep Kellen from scoring. I did pretty good too."

"Of course you did. I took Roscoe out to the stables last night."

Noel couldn't stop the wicked smile that took over her face with a swiftness. Roscoe liked the reindeer, like they were a novelty or something, but the reindeer did not share the sentiment. "How did the reindeer react?"

"About like you would have expected. I've never seen Comet run so fast. He looked like a comet last night."

"It did him some good then."

"Did me good too; I laughed so hard, I cried."

"I bet you did. How did the other reindeer react?"

"Donner tried to act like he wasn't scared, but it was a lost cause. Roscoe cornered Vixen. I thought Vixen was going to pass out. I just knew she was going to get hurt, and you were going to kill me. But, then Roscoe gave her a great big bear hug. I think he made a new friend for life. Vixen couldn't get enough cuddle time after that. I always knew there was something wrong with that reindeer."

"There's nothing wrong with Vixen. She just likes physical affection."

"From a polar bear," Shepherd pushed.

"This is coming from the kid who works best with elves."

"The elves are hard workers, especially when they have someone to direct them."

"There is that and the fact that you hold the sole title of toy tester."

"Yeah, that too," Shepherd laughed.

For someone with so much wisdom beyond his years, Shepherd was still very much a kid at heart. Noel suspected that he always would be.

"So, when can we expect you back? Roscoe is beside himself. I almost believe that bear thinks he's your father."

Noel laughed. "I don't know. I have no idea how long training might take, but it doesn't feel like I've learned anything yet."

"Well, that sucks."

"Yeah, it does."

"It buys you more time with the son of a Clause hater, though, doesn't it?" Shepherd teased.

"Ha, ha, very funny."

"Do his parents know you're spending so much time with him?"

"Who said I was spending so much time with him?"

"Who said you weren't? Ethan is not going to be easy to deal with when he finds out, and he will find out."

"I'm not seeking him out or anything. He's just there, in the same place. How can we be faulted for that?" Noel had meant to sound detached, but she sounded more desperate instead.

"Don't be mad, Noel. I'm not saying what you're doing is wrong. I'm not saying he's a bad guy, just that his dad will make you both regret it."

"What do you want me to do? Go out of my way to avoid Kellen?"

"No, not even that. I just want you to be prepared."

"Ok, fine."

"I'm sorry, Noel."

"Noel, lunch is ready," Nickolas called from inside the house.

"I've got to go. I love you, Shepherd."

"Love you too, and Noel... I miss you." Shepherd said before hanging up.

# Chapter Eighteen

The next morning, Kellen was at the cave bright and early. "Come on, sleepy head. Time to get up and run. Let's go."

"I don't want to. Go away."

"Not going to happen. Get up, or I'll get you up."

"You're worse than Aunt Mary," Noel grumbled as she rolled out of bed. Thank heavens her pajamas weren't embarrassing.

"Hurry up. If you aren't out in one minute, Princess and I are leaving without you."

Noel pulled on a pair of sweats and stretched as quickly as she dared. As soon as she stepped out into the cold, Kellen was off and running. She had to rush to catch up.

They were moving at a slow and steady trot while Princess ran circles around them. Noel had finally gotten over the initial soreness left behind by all the exercise. She was moving with ease, but her mind was anything but at ease. Something Shepherd had said the day before stuck with her. "Aren't you worried someone will see us out here running?" Noel asked Kellen.

"Why worry? Is it a crime to run now?"

"Don't be ridiculous. I'm serious. What if someone sees us together and tells your dad?"

"I don't care."

"Why not?"

"Because I don't care about his opinion."

"But, he's your dad."

"And, he's wrong this time."

"But-"

"But nothing. Give me one reason why he should be holding on to that grudge. You did hear the sermon yesterday, right?"

"You were there?"

"Yes, I was there. Did you think my family didn't go to church just because he doesn't like the Clauses?"

"I didn't see you there."

"If you didn't see me, I must not have been there. Is that it?"

"No, I was just surprised."

"Why?"

"I told you. I was surprised, because I didn't see you. What is with you? Why are you so testy this morning?"

"Why are you so worried about being seen with me?"

"I've never met your dad, but I know he hates my mom. I'm just not sure how he will react."

"He wouldn't hurt you if that's what you're thinking. He's not a monster."

"I'm sorry. I didn't mean to insinuate… He did attack the North Pole, though, didn't he? I thought Dad sent him back here after they were stopped. That's what you said."

"That's what Uncle Noah says, but he didn't actually hurt anyone while he was there. He didn't go through with it."

"What would he do then? If he found out you had been out here?"

"Probably yell at me. He wouldn't come after you. Most likely he'd pretend you just don't exist. That's how he deals with your aunt and her children. He barely tolerates Coach Declan. If Coach Declan weren't one of Uncle Noah's best friends, he'd probably pretend he didn't exist either."

"That doesn't sound so bad. Why was Noah so concerned that your dad knew about that day we found Princess?"

"Dad wouldn't take it out on you; that doesn't mean he won't take it out on me."

"You said he'd just yell."

"I did. He will. Do you have any idea how hard it is to be the family who don't like the Clauses? Everyone loves Mrs. Star, and since she uncovered the origin of the feud, people have been letting it go. Everyone but my dad. We aren't allowed to let it go. It's like we are detached from everyone else. We pretend like everything is ok, but it's not. I feel like the outsider even when I'm with my friends."

"I'm so sorry."

"Don't be. I must sound pathetic to you. You live in the North Pole with only your family. Do you even have friends?"

"I have friends," Noel said defensively. "Angel and Gloria are my best friends. I just didn't get to see them every day at school."

"How often do you get to see them?"

"Once or twice a year. It's harder to track Gloria down. Angel and I had fixed location homes, but Gloria moves around."

"Why does she move so much?"

"Her parents' work has them moving a lot."

"What do they do?"

"The same thing all Clauses are expected to do."

"What's that?"

Noel looked at Kellen as if he had lost his mind. Maybe he had. Surely, he had heard the circumstances that started the feud. Hadn't he? "Don't you know what started the feud?"

"Yeah. Do the Clauses still do that?"

"Yes!"

"You're training with your aunts is, it…"

"Yes."

"You're training to fight vampires… I can't see it."

"If my dad gets his way, you will."

"What does that mean?"

"Nothing. We better hurry up, or you'll be late for school." It was a cop out, but Noel didn't feel like talking about it.

Aunt Mary slowly upped Noel's run mileage until she was running five miles twice a day. She still did intense physical workouts with Aunt Star, but at least the two teachers had finally begun to teach. They killed two birds with one stone. As they taught her to fight, they also recalled lessons that had been shared with them or they had learned on their own. They inserted little tidbits of advice here and there. Not that Noel was picking up on any of it. It all stuck with her about as well as the fighting techniques did.

Day after day, Noel got her butt kicked by her two ancient aunts. She returned to the cave battered and bruised and had to turn around and teach Princess to hunt.

Teaching Princess was a slow process mainly because Princess had no desire to hunt. Why would she? She got fed well and didn't have to work for it. Why pick up hunting when you could play all day?

The rest of her evenings were spent doing some thinking and a lot of praying. Noel prayed and studied her Bible. She studied and prayed, but she still didn't feel a calling for her life to change course. She wasn't a vampire hunter.

After an especially late night pleading with Princess to try hunting, Noel was sparing with Aunt Star. Noel thought she was doing pretty good. Aunt Star had not pinned her once yet. Of course, she had not pinned Aunt Star either.

"Noel, you've got to focus. All you're doing is holding your own," Aunt Star scolded.

"What's wrong with that?"

"You're going to tire out. The vampire won't. If all you do is hold your own, all your doing is delaying your death."

"Ouch, take it easy on the kid, Star," Uncle Declan said from his spectator's position on the couch.

"This is life or death, Declan. She hasn't even advanced to taking on both of us yet."

"She's come a long way for someone who never wanted to do this in the first place, baby."

"Tell me again why the rink is closed today," Star demanded.

"Last hockey game of the season is tonight. It's a big deal. You know this, babe."

"Couldn't you find somewhere else to go?"

"Nope. I like watching you fight. There's nothing sexier."

"Ugh, Uncle Declan," Noel moaned.

"Hey, I'm on your side, kid. Can't you let her off to get ready for the game tonight. Do the rest of us a favor so that we don't have to smell her."

"I wasn't planning on going," Noel admitted.

"What? You can't miss the last game. Go on and get changed."

"Declan, you are not in charge of her training," Aunt Star growled.

"It's only an hour early, Star," Aunt Mary stepped in. "We all need the time to get ready. Calder, Harding, and Trumble have been avidly reminding me that I can't miss the game. The only thing those boys like more than hockey is fighting. They are definitely Vivienne's kids."

"No one who's anyone misses the last game of the season," Uncle Declan announced proudly.

"I'm not anyone here in the South Pole," Noel pointed out. Mostly she did it to bug Uncle Declan, but she wasn't all that interested in the game either.

"You're my niece. Now go get cleaned up," Uncle Declan ordered as if the matter had been settled.

Noel looked at Aunt Star for confirmation. Aunt Star shrugged at Noel and sat down in Uncle Declan's lap. Uncle Declan kissed her neck, and Noel wasted no time getting out of there before things could get any more personal. A bit of magic had her inside the cave in a blink.

"I'm so glad you came tonight," Angel said seated next to Noel in the stands. This is the jock social event of the year. It's like their version of Mom's dances, except Mom usually has more than one a year."

"Angel, we're not jocks," Noel pointed out.

"You almost are. You help Dad out at the rink."

"I don't always do that."

"You do sometimes, and it's almost always with Kellen Nickola."

"Angel, shut up! Isn't his dad here somewhere?"

"Oh, relax. Ethan Nickola would never sit close enough to a Clause to overhear what they were saying. I think he's… Yep, there he is," Angel said pointing across the ice to the bleachers furthest from where she and Noel sat.

Ethan Nickola was too far to see clearly, but Noel was curious. She had seen picture of him as a teen, but she had never seen him as an adult. Noel sent a jolt of magic to her eyes increasing magnification.

Wow, he really did look like Kellen. Noel knew for certain that Kellen looked exactly like his dad had at that same age, but he still looked exactly like his dad, the way his dad looked today. Maybe that was a sign that Kellen was going to age well.

Looks were all Kellen had in common with his dad. Ethan Nickola sat as far away from the Clauses as he could get. Kellen Nickola joined Noel every weekday morning to run together. He also claimed he was going to be more involved in teaching Princess to hunt after hockey season ended. I guess they'd know by next week, if he really meant that.

"That's Kellen, number 77," Angel said pointing.

Noel nodded.

"We'll see if all those lessons you've been helping out with are doing him any good. Hey, is he still running with you?"

"Angel! Stop, you don't know who might be listening."

"Oh, please. It's so loud in here, no one can hear a word I'm saying but you. I was just going to say if he's coming over anyway, he should return the favor. You helped him with hockey. He could help you with training. You know?"

"What does he know about vampire hunting?"

"What do you know about hockey?"

"Touché. Still, I think I can do without his help."

"Suit yourself, but if it were me, I'd jump at the chance to get up close and personal with Kellen Nickola"

Noel didn't know how to react to that profession, so she chose to ignore it. "Who are the other players?"

That got Angel talking. She pointed out each player and told a brief history for each one. There were none she was so taken with as Kellen, but the boy she was most taken with was sitting two rows down and kept looking back at Angel.

"Who is that guy down there who has been eye flirting with you all night?" Noel asked.

"Eye flirting? What do you know about flirting, Noel Clause?"

"It sounded better in my head."

"I certainly hope so."

"So, who is he?"

"That's Justin Thomas." Noel had noticed the way Angel had looked at him all night, but it was that dreamy voice that gave her away. She liked this guy.

"Tell me about him."

"Why? He doesn't play hockey."

"Only hockey players are worth talking about?"

"No, but tonight's about the hockey."

"For your dad maybe. I want to hear about Justin Thomas."

"What do you want to know?"

"Give me anything you've got."

"He's seventeen years old. He's a junior in high school. He has an older sister who graduated last year. She's two years older than him. He does choir, and he's really good at it. Sometimes he sings solos at church. He played little league hockey. Dad says he was pretty good too, but he quit when he got to high school to do choir. I guess he likes singing more."

"Is he nice?"

"Yeah, I mean I've never seen him be mean to anyone. He's not a bully or anything."

"Does he have a girlfriend?"

"I don't think so. Why? Are you interested?"

"Me? No, I don't even know the guy."

"Why did you ask then?"

"Don't you like him?"

"Me?" Angel paused for a minute deciding how much to tell. "Ok, yes. I do, but he doesn't see me like that."

"He definitely sees you. He couldn't quit looking at you tonight."

"He has looked up here a lot, hasn't he? We're friends, I think."

"You think?"

"Yeah, I think we're friends, but I know we aren't more than that. He sees me as some dumb kid."

"Why would he see you that way. He's not much older than you, and you are not dumb."

"Not dumb in the literal sense. He thinks I'm silly, frivolous."

"You're not silly. You're fun."

"You're my best friend. You have to say that."

"Angel, because I'm your best friend, I can tell you the truth. You're fun, like your mom, and everyone loves your mom."

"They do love Mom."

The rest of the game went fast as they talked about boys.

Chapter Nineteen

That night Angel stayed with Noel. After all it was Friday, and they had fallen into an enjoyable pattern of Angel staying over every weekend. The girls hadn't been sure at first if Aunt Star would let Angel stay every weekend, but so far, she had. Really, it wasn't even a question anymore.

The girls were up into the wee hours of morning talking and eating chocolate pudding. Ok, the pudding might have been a little juvenile, but who could resist the cool, smooth, creamy pudding?

Obviously, they were in no hurry to get up the next morning. Noel had registered the cold at one point and realized that they had fallen asleep above the covers, yet she couldn't muster up the effort to slide under the covers.

Sometime later, Noel didn't know how much time, she registered the deep male voice saying, "Hey, Princess. Is that lazy Clause not out of bed yet?"

The voice was familiar, not at all threatening, so Noel moaned for the speaker to go away then curled into a ball to ward off the cold. Before Noel could drift back into a deep sleep, Angel was screaming and stripping the covers from beneath Noel.

"I'm sorry. I'm sorry. I'll-I'm..."

"Get up, Noel! Noel! Get up right now!" Angel shrieked. "There was a boy in here with us. I thought no one could get in here, like a locked door."

"Unless they've been here before. It was just Kellen."

"What was he doing here?"

"I don't know."

"I came to run," Kellen answered from outside the cave.

"It's Saturday. You never come to run on Saturday," Noel pointed out.

"I have extra time now that hockey season is over. Could you two get dressed?"

"We are dressed."

"Noel, we're in our pajamas," Angel protested drawing out the last word.

"It's not like he's never seen pajamas before."

"He doesn't even have sisters at home."

"So what? Kellen, go away. It's too early to run."

"It's nearly 9:00, and I'm not going back home anyway," he replied.

Noel groaned and fell out of bed. She forced her eyes open enough to find a pair of sweats. "Are you coming?" she asked Angel.

"Where?"

"Running."

"You mean those crazy five mile runs that Mama and Aunt Mary have you doing?" Angel asked incredulously. "I don't think so."

"I don't blame you. Unfortunately, I don't have the same option. We'll be back."

"Take your time. I need to get home to work on a big project anyway." It was a project that Angel hadn't mentioned last night. It was a little too convenient if you asked Noel. "You two have fun," Angel suggested with a mischievous smile as Noel was tying her cleats.

"What's with your cousin?" Kellen asked once they were out of hearing distance from the cave.

"Who knows. What are you doing here?"

"I told you I came to run with you."

"I know you said that, but why did you come to run on a Saturday? You rarely show up to run on a Saturday."

"I thought you ran everyday regardless. I can leave if you would rather."

"It's not that. You didn't say anything yesterday. You scared Angel to death."

"Yeah, tell her I'm sorry about that."

"So, why did you not tell me you were coming today?"

"Does it matter?"

"I don't guess so, but at least Angel would have been expecting you."

Kellen didn't say anything for a long time. "I had a fight with my dad."

"I'm sorry. What were you fighting about?"

Kellen snorted. "What do my dad and I not fight about? He just said some stuff."

"Stuff?"

"Yeah, do you want to work with Princess today? Maybe I can help you teach her to hunt."

"Sure."

Angel was long gone when they got back from their run, so Noel and Kellen went straight to work with Princess. Princess was pulling her stubborn act, but two could play that game.

"You're not getting any bottles until you've tried. You have to learn to do this," Noel scolded.

"Maybe you could use the bottles as incentive to get her to try," Kellen suggested.

Noel just stared at him. How was that helpful? They were trying to get her off the bottles, so if she did a good job, they'd give the bottles back again? That didn't even make sense. It was counterproductive.

"Just for a while, until she gets the hang of it," he added sheepishly.

"Fine," Noel sighed. "If you do a good job, you can have one bottle. One."

Princess huffed, apparently not too enthused by the incentive of only one bottle. She pushed to her feet and trotted out of the cave as if anxious to get the ordeal over with. She still didn't seem to be in a cooperative mood.

Noel and Kellen followed her out and sat down on the ice next to where Princess had plopped down. "Now just watch the water hole for signs of a seal the way I showed you," Noel instructed.

They sat there. There was no way to know if Princess was looking for signs or even understood, but still they sat. Eventually a seal popped up out of the water walked around the hole and dove back in. Princess didn't react. She didn't so much as flinch.

"Ok," Kellen whispered, "now all you need to do is silently creep up to the hole and wait. When the seal comes back up for air, sink your teeth and claws into it."

Princess began belly crawling. Wow! Maybe she just preferred Kellen's direction. That was something they would definitely be having a talk about later, but in the meantime, at least she was doing it.

She approached the hole and waited patiently. At last the seal resurfaced and Princess attacked. Princess sure got her claws in deep, because the seal took Princess back into the water.

"Princess!" Kellen screamed. He and Noel both ran up to the hole. The water was tinged with red, blood.

"No," Noel dropped to her knees. "No, no, no."

Noel crashed through the surface spitting water everywhere. Kellen grabbed her and hauled her out of the water. He never slowed down or even put her down. He ran straight to the cave, with Noel close on his heels.

He laid her down on the bed and started searching her body franticly for injuries.

"She's fine. She's fine. Not even a scratch. It must have all been the seal's blood."

The bed was soaked now, but Noel didn't much care. She quickly and efficiently used magic to dry off Kellen and Princess then suggested they get some breakfast. Princess had given a genuine effort today, so Noel didn't begrudge her the bottles one bit. While Kellen gave Princess the bottles, Noel cooked up some eggs and bacon for herself and Kellen.

"You do realize it's past noon, right? It's a little late for breakfast," Kellen teased.

"If you don't want it, you don't have to eat it."

"I didn't say that. If you cook it, I'll eat it, no matter what time of day... I heard you were at the game last night."

"What?" How had he heard that? Who had overheard her and Angel. She told Angel to keep quiet. "Who told you that?"

"Dad."

"What?"

"Yeah, that's sort of what started this morning's fight."

Noel sat down at the table next to Kellen and asked, "So, what did he say?"

"You don't want to hear all that."

"I can handle it. Hit me with it."

"Are you sure. It's not nice."

"I'm a big girl."

"Well, he said that you didn't have to be sitting with the Clauses for him to know exactly who you are, because you are the spitting image of your dad."

"He's got me there," Noel admitted. "What else? That's not what you fought about."

"He said the daughter of Wynter Clause had some nerve coming down here…"

Noel waited, but Kellen didn't continue. "You didn't fight with him over that, I hope, so what happened next?"

"He said someone should teach you a lesson."

He threatened her? For a second Noel forgot to breath. She had never met this man before in her life. Why would he want to threaten her? How could he possibly hate her already?

"Noel?" That jolted Noel back to the present; Kellen rarely used her first name.

"What did you say then?" Noel asked trying to buy a few minutes.

"I said someone should teach him a lesson. We both yelled for a while. Then I called him a violent bigot, and I left. I never believed that he would actually hurt you, not physically anyway, but maybe I gave him too much credit."

Kellen shoved his empty plate away and stood up. Man, that boy could eat fast! He threw the wet blankets and sheets off the bed and sat down with his back against the head board. He didn't say anything else, and Noel didn't know what to say. So, they sat in silence while Noel continued to eat and tried to absorb everything she had just heard.

When she had finished and put the dishes in the sink, Noel sat down next to Kellen and softly asked, "Do you think he would act on it for real?"

"What?" He gave her a startled look before understanding set in. He reached across his body and pulled her head down to rest on his left shoulder, and he gently laid his own head atop hers. "No, he would never do anything. It's too dangerous. It would be him against the whole of South Pole. He can't fight off everyone, and if he went after you, that's exactly what he would have to do. I've told you before, everyone loves your aunt."

"Everyone but your dad."

"Don't worry about him. His approval isn't worth it."

"My mom thinks so."

"Really?"

"Yeah, she doesn't talk about him much, but I can tell she still has hope that they'll be friends again someday."

"That's crazy."

"That's Mom."

"It must be reassuring having someone who loves so unselfishly."

"I never thought about it before, but yeah, it is."

"I think you must be a lot like her. Look at all you're willing to go through for Princess, for your dad. You'd be a good friend to have."

"We're friends, aren't we?"

"Yeah, we are."

They sat there like that on the bed and talked for hours. It wasn't the same as when she sat for hours talking with Angel or Gloria, but it was nice just the same.

## Chapter Twenty

The next week was, in Noel's book, a success. Aunt Star had taught Noel how to make glitter into a weapon. It was fascinating how magic could make something so beautiful into something so dangerous. If an army had a gas for any given situation, Noel could do the same thing in glitter now thanks to Aunt Star. Noel hadn't put it to any practical use during sparing, but she knew how to do it. Glitter could be used for a rather inspiring explosion as well, even though Aunt Mary pointed out that explosions were not discreet.

Plus, Aunt Star had some of the coolest throwing Stars! They came in beautiful colors and, of course, had very girly designs. They shimmered too. Aunt

Mary gave Noel a set of throwing stars that were plain, a dull metal color.

Aunt Star leaned close to Noel's ear and whispered, "You can sit down later with Angel and decorate them."

Noel's sparing skills showed little improvement, if any. She never managed to take Aunt Star or Aunt Mary down, but Princess managed to tear a chunk off a seal before it got away.

Kellen had been coming over every afternoon after school to help. He said he couldn't stand the idea of going home early. Day after day they took Princess out to hunt. She had the concept down. She just couldn't overpower the seal long enough for a take down. Were they starting her out with too big a prey? Was she just not ready yet? Maybe she wasn't strong enough yet; was she malnourished?

Friday, it happened. Princess latched onto the seal with her powerful jaw and began to shake like a dog with a bone. It was hilarious to watch. The seal managed to escape but not before Princess had torn away a hunk of flesh. Princess wasted no time in chewing up and swallowing her prize.

"That's it, Princess! You did it!"

"That was so perfect!"

"Maybe now that she has a taste of what she's missing, that will be the key to success," Kellen speculated.

"That was disgusting," Angel said from behind them.

"Don't say that. You'll discourage her. Don't listen to her, Princess. You did that exactly right," Kellen cooed at Princess.

"When did you get here?" Noel asked Angel.

"Just in time to see that sweet baby turn into a vicious polar."

"She is a polar bear," Kellen pointed out the obvious.

"So, have you two been running again?"

"Not since this morning. We're trying to teach Princess to hunt," Noel told her.

"Ah, I think I'll wait inside. Make sure you clean her up first."

The three of them hung out all weekend long only interrupted by hunting trips and running sessions. Princess had not had any more success, but it was still a triumph. Evening runs were still the most peaceful. Sometimes Kellen would run with her, and sometimes she would run by herself. Those were the nights she spent really considering her options and trying hard to listen for God's will.

Noel was no closer to a decision. Rather, she was no closer to the decision Dad wanted for her, yet it was still a perfect weekend.

That perfect weekend came to a screeching halt when Aunt Mary showed up Saturday morning and sent Angel home early.

"Noel, I need to talk to you about something. Sit down, please. This isn't going to be easy for me to say, even harder for you to hear. Something's happened at home."

At Noel's home or Aunt Mary's home?

Aunt Mary took a deep breath and continued, "It's Roscoe, he-he's gone, baby."

"No!"

Aunt Mary had come straight here after Dad called her, and she told Noel what had happened. Noel heard every word, yet it was like she was in a daze. Like she was watching the whole scene from afar.

"I can go with you if you want," Aunt Mary offered.

"No, no, I just need to be alone," Noel managed to choke out.

Aunt Mary left then. Noel was alone. She stared straight ahead. There were no tears rolling down her face. She had no tears at all. She couldn't cry, not even for her lifelong companion. Her chest was tight, making it hard to breath. She didn't move. She didn't blink. She just sat there waiting for it to sink in.

"Rise and shine, girls," Kellen called from outside.

What right did he have to be so cheerful when everything was falling apart all around Noel. Princess whimpered.

"Princess? Clause?" Kellen walked in and spotted Noel sitting on the edge of the bed staring into nothingness. "What's happened?"

"It's Roscoe."

"Who?"

"My family's pet polar."

"Oh, yeah, I remember. Is he ok?"

"He's gone."

Kellen didn't say another word. He sat down next to her and hugged her. Noel buried her face against his chest. She wanted to hide the shame that she couldn't even cry for Roscoe.

It was a long time before Noel was able to find her voice again, but when she did, the flood gates finally opened up. Tears cascaded down her face in a torrent.

"I wasn't even there. He was my lifelong companion, and I wasn't even there when he died."

"I'm sure he knew you loved him. How did it happen?"

"He was old. He had already lived longer than most polars. We knew it was coming, but it isn't any easier. Aunt Mary said it was peaceful. It happened in the night. He was asleep."

"Can't you poof yourself to the North Pole, be with your family right now?"

"Go with me?" Noel wasn't sure why she asked him that. All she knew is that she couldn't stand the idea of going anywhere alone right now.

"Sure, I will." Kellen stood up and pulled Noel into his arms, where she laid her head against his chest again.

One second they were in the cave, and the next second they were in the North Pole.

"Noel," Mom said.

When Noel looked up Mom's eyes were bloodshot. Her face was red and streaked with tears. She reached out and pulled Noel into her arms. They stood there in each other's arms as they balled like babies over the bear they both loved like a part of the family. Dad walked up and put a consoling hand on each of their backs and rubbed soothing circles. Somewhere in the back of Noel's mind it registered that Shepherd was sitting on the couch, silent and stoic.

Mom looked to Kellen and thanked him, "Thank you for bringing her home."

"It wasn't me. My magic-I mean I can't," Kellen stumbled through his words.

"You did more than you know," Mom said pulling him into their embrace.

"Shepherd, go get the girls some cookies and hot chocolate," Dad instructed.

"Anthony, cookies aren't the answer to everything," Mom responded tersely.

"They couldn't hurt."

"I could use some cookies," Noel said.

Mom looked at Noel and nodded.

Shepherd came back with enough hot chocolate and cookies for everyone. Mom took only a mug of hot chocolate and sat down on the love seat. Noel took three cookies and sat down next to Mom. Dad didn't take a single cookie, which spoke volumes about his state of mind. Dad didn't turn down cookies. Noel was sure she had never seen Dad turn down a single cookie.

"Thank you," Kellen said as he took a mug of hot chocolate and a cookie.

Shepherd took a mug for himself and sat back down on the couch. Dad sat down next to him and clapped him on the shoulder. "You're doing fine, son, but let me be the man of the house. It's still my job to take care of you. I'm here now."

Now? Where had Dad been? For that matter where were Papa and Gam? What was happening to Noel's family in her absence?

Shepherd nodded and leaned into Dad's embrace. Kellen, who looked nervous, sat down in Dad's recliner. It wasn't like Dad would be needing it any time soon.

Noel swallowed hard and asked, "Where is he?"

"Papa and I buried him earlier. You, your mom, and brother didn't need to see him like that," Dad said.

That explained where Dad had been earlier, but where was Papa now? And, what about Gam? Noel made eye contact with Kellen, and he gave her a tentative smile. Kellen was in the North Pole. Papa and Gam were missing, and Roscoe was gone. How had the world turned so topsy turvy?

All the hot chocolate was gone by the time Papa and Gam walked in the door along with the aroma of garlic and tomatoes. What was that they were eating this early in the morning. Surely it was too early to eat.

"Everyone come to the kitchen," Gam ordered authoritatively. "I know we're all heart broken, but you can't stop eating. Let's go, every one of you."

"Who are you?" Papa asked coming to a stop inside the living room.

"Kellen Nickola."

"He's Ethan's son, Dad. Noah's nephew," Mom answered when Papa didn't react right away.

"Oh, yes. It's nice to meet you, son, but can I ask what you're doing here?"

"I um…"

"He brought Noel," Mom filled in.

"Good, good. Come eat with us."

Mom kissed Noel's cheek then stood up. She patted Kellen's shoulder on her way to the kitchen. Dad stood up and offered his hand to help Shepherd up. Dad walked into the kitchen next. Papa wrapped Shepherd in a hug, and they followed behind Dad. Noel and Kellen were the only two left in the living room, and Noel wondered what this must all look like to Kellen.

"We must look pathetic," she voiced.

"Nah, it would kill me if we lost Princess, and I'm surrounded by more people in the South Pole than you are here. He was a part of the family. I get it." Kellen got up and moved to the love seat next to Noel. "Are you hungry?"

"Not really."

"It's getting late. You should eat something."

"What time is it?"

"Almost one."

"How can it be that late?"

"You're upset. Try to eat something?"

Noel nodded, so Kellen took her by the hand and led her to the kitchen. Every eye in the room drifted in their direction when they walked in. Mom, who was already sitting at the table, smiled a weary looking smile and turned back around. Gam went back to work putting food and drinks on the table, and Papa went back to work setting plates, napkins, and forks on the table.  Dad was hovering over Mom still on his feet. He kissed Noel's head and whispered into her hairline, "I love you."

"Love you too," Noel choked.

"Shepherd, scoot down one, and let Kellen sit by Noel," Gam said patting Shepherd on the shoulder.

Shepherd who had not taken his eyes off of Noel and Kellen, more specifically their joined hands, moved down, but narrowed his eyes in Kellen's direction. "How old are you anyway?" he asked.

"Shepherd," Mom admonished.

"It's ok, Mrs. Clause. I'm nineteen," Kellen answered.

"You're older than Noel?"

"Yes."

"Where were you when your dad attacked the North Pole?"

"Shepherd that is enough," Dad said firmly.

Noel could not believe that Shepherd was being so confrontational. It wasn't like him at all.

"I don't know. I was barely two, if I was that old. It's not something that people in the South Pole talk much about. Everything I know about it, I learned from Uncle Noah."

Shepherd opened his mouth as if to spit more venom, but Papa cleared his throat instead. "You remind me of your uncle. He's a fierce friend, and he never backs down when he knows he's right. Those are admirable qualities."

"Thank you, sir."

Gam had homemade lasagna, garlic bread, and salad, enough to feed a small army or at least a family double or even triple their size. Noel ate on autopilot without ever really tasting the food.

After everyone finished eating, Noel wandered out to the backyard, with Kellen shadowing her every move. The backyard seemed so expansive and empty without Roscoe there. Noel stood there replaying in her mind every game she had ever played growing up with Roscoe. When she couldn't remember any more, she started walking.

Before she knew where she was going, she was down by the stables. The reindeer were calm, quiet. They were subdued as if they could sense the somber mood. Maybe they could. She always believed that those reindeer were extremely intuitive when it came to the family.

"These are the famous reindeer then, huh?" Kellen said softly.

"Blitzen, Dancer, and Vixen are the three girls. The boys are Comet, Donner, Prancer, and Cupid. Donner is the leader, and this is Cupid's last year before he retires."

"Who will take his place?" Kellen asked.

Noel led him around to the new fawns' stables. "These are the only two fawns ready to move up. This is Captain, and this one's Cookie. She'll be the one to take Cupid's place next year."

"How did she get her name?"

"She really loves cookies. She's forever stealing cookies from Dad."

"Oh."

Noel went to work feeding the reindeer. She wasn't sure that anyone had remembered, and she could use the normalcy.

"So, your brother doesn't like me much," Kellen commented after the last reindeer was fed.

"It's nothing personal. He worries about me. He's not really himself today either. None of us are."

"That's understandable."

"There's nothing else I can do here."

"Do you want to go back home?"

"This is my home."

"I'm sorry."

"I miss him already."

Kellen looked around helplessly before saying, "I don't know what to do."

Noel was feeling all alone without her closest friend in all the world. What she craved right now more than anything was contact. She would settle for any contact she could get, a bear hug, a reindeer cuddle, or a human embrace, so she stepped forward and hugged Kellen. He didn't hesitate to return the hug. He held her tight until she could no longer feel her toes and her fingers tingled.

After telling her family goodbye, Noel and Kellen returned to the South Pole. Aunt Star was waiting inside the cave when they got there.

"Hey, precious. How is everyone doing?" she asked.

"Mom is a mess. I guess she's reacting the same way I am for the most part. Shepherd is trying to play Mr. tough guy, and it's just making him mean," Noel answered.

"He'll come around. He just needs time to process... Noah called the house earlier looking for you," Aunt Star told Kellen. "Your dad has been looking for you, and he's pretty upset. You better hurry home."

Kellen looked at Noel but didn't say a word.

"I'll stay with her. You go on."

Noel nodded before Kellen would make a move. He gave her hand one last squeeze and left.

"Do you want to talk about it?" Aunt Star asked.

"No, I'm just tired."

Aunt Star pulled a pair of pajamas from a bag that Noel had not noticed before. After they had both changed into pajamas, Aunt Star curled up in bed with Noel and stayed with her the whole night through. That was what Noel loved most about Aunt Star. She just knew intuitively what Noel needed most. Maybe it was the bond they shared. Maybe it was wisdom gained from experience. Whatever it was, Noel would always be grateful for Aunt Star and the bond they shared.

Losing a pet would be hard on anyone, but there wasn't much companionship in the North Pole. That just made losing a beloved pet harder. Aunt Star understood that in a way that only a Clause could.

## Chapter Twenty-One

The next day, Noel went through the motions at church, yet she felt like she was still in a fog. Aunt Mary and Aunt Star both insisted that Noel take the next week off. According to her aunts she needed time to process and accept.

She didn't see Kellen the next week either. It was like he had dropped off the face of the earth. He didn't come to visit. He didn't come to help teach Princess. He just… didn't.

Noel spent the week focused on teaching Princess and focused on reflecting. By the end of the week she was even smiling again. Not much, but even a small smile was a step in the right direction. At last Noel came to a decision. She had to buckle down and master this vampire hunting thing so that she and

Dad could talk it out. She needed some finality on the subject. She couldn't just keep flapping in the wind. Otherwise, it would drive her mad.

Angel came over Friday night to see if she could stay the weekend with Noel. Of course, Noel said yes. It would be nice to have one of her best friends with her.

"How's the hunting thing going for Princess?" Angel asked.

"She's getting better. I think she misses Kellen. We haven't seen him all week," Noel answered.

"You won't either. He's grounded for disappearing last weekend. It could be worse. I think his dad knows he was with you. He just can't prove it. That's what everybody is saying at school. His dad was mad. He grounded Kellen for two weeks."

"That isn't fair."

"Nope, but that's Kellen's dad. Nothing's fair when it comes to the Clauses, and as far as he's concerned, your mom is the worst of the lot."

"You're a part of that lot," Noel pointed out hotly.

"I know. I'm just telling you the way Kellen's dad thinks."

"It isn't fair."

"No, it isn't, but Kellen must have known what would happen when he left with you."

"I didn't mean to get him in trouble."

"I didn't say you did, but he knew he'd get in trouble."

That was a lot to think about. It made what Kellen did for her that much kinder. It also made Noel feel guilty. She'd asked him to go with her. She hadn't wanted to go alone, and she had asked for what she had no right to take. Kellen went with her to the North Pole knowing he'd get in trouble, and then he got hounded by her brother for his trouble.

It was Wednesday when it happened. Noel was sparing with Aunt Star and faked her out. Aunt Star was expecting a right jab, but Noel swept her legs out from beneath her instead. In less than a second, Aunt Star was pinned to the ground with a magically ineffectual stake aimed at her heart.

"Good. Now do it again," Aunt Mary demanded, but Noel didn't care.

She leapt to her feet and started jumping for joy. "I did it. I did it. I did it. I did it. I did it!" Soon her jumping morphed into a victory dance complete with glitter raining down.

Suddenly Aunt Star's arms wrapped around Noel's neck from behind. "Never stop to celebrate, the next vampire to come out of the shadows has you right where he wants you."

Noel sighed and Aunt Star set up to go another round. Noel managed to pin Aunt Star three more times that day and five more by Friday.

"Next week, you'll spar with me," Aunt Mary announced. "Star is rusty."

Aunt Star tried to look affronted but ended up shrugging her reluctant agreement instead. Noel was pretty psyched up after her recent success and actually looked forward to taking on Aunt Mary. They all knew that Aunt Mary was the real challenge. It wasn't that Aunt Star was soft, but she had not been hunting in about sixteen years.

Noel wanted to tell someone about her progress, but there wasn't anyone to tell. Angel was in the middle of some big school project that had kept her busy all week long. Noel was starting to realize that was almost always the case with Angel, and Kellen was still MIA, grounded if Angel was right.

Funny, how quickly she had come to think of him as a friend, especially when she had been so reluctant the first time they met. Noel had been afraid that he would be exactly like his father, that he would hate her and her family. That wasn't the case at all. Kellen couldn't have been less like his dad if he tried, which Noel thought that sometimes he did.

Chances were Noel would never go running or just sit and talk to Kellen ever again. Oh, she'd see him no doubt. The South Pole wasn't large enough for them to avoid each other forever. They'd see each other in passing or from across the sanctuary at church. Surely though, Kellen wouldn't want to spend any more time with Noel now that he'd seen exactly what his time spent would get him.

She couldn't blame him either. Her time in the South Pole was limited. When she finally managed to finish her training, she would be returning to the North Pole. They'd spend the rest of their lives a world apart. It felt like they were already a world apart.

It was a horrible, hopeless feeling, and that's why it surprised her so much when Kellen showed up at the cave Saturday morning. "Clause, wake up. I've been paroled."

"Kellen?" Noel answered sitting straight up in bed.

"Yeah, who'd you think it was. Where's Angel?"

"She has a group project she's been working on. They're all going to meet today to finish it."

"Want to go for a run before we work with Princess?"

"Sure, I guess."

"Ok, we'll be outside. Come on, Princess."

Noel threw on sweats and cleats, eager to be outside with Kellen and Princess. She practically bolted out of the cave. "What are you doing here?"

"We always run on Saturday morning."

"I know, but weren't you grounded?"

"I was, but I told you I've been paroled."

"Aren't you afraid that you'll get grounded again?"

"No. No one is going to see us way out here anyway, so let's get going."

Noel smiled as Kellen took off at a slow jog, and she hurried to keep up.

"So, where do your parents think you are?" Noel wondered.

"Dad wasn't up when I left. Mom called not long after I left the house, and I told her that I was going to Uncle Noah's."

"Won't she be mad when she finds out you lied?"

"I didn't lie. I'll go see Uncle Noah when I leave here, so I'm still going to Uncle Noah's. I'm just not there yet."

"It's still a lie. Will Noah be upset when he finds out you used him as an alibi?"

"Nah, it wouldn't be the first time. Uncle Noah and Aunt Lorelei are used to it."

"What if something bad happened and no one could find you?"

"What could happen?"

"I don't know. You could be attacked by a wild animal."

"Nah, I never used to go out on my own in unpopulated areas. I didn't start coming out here until you moved in. Now I've got a polar bear on my side. What animal would be stupid enough to attack?"

"I don't think that wild animals are known for thinking logically, and as for Princess, she's hardly some fierce protector."

"But, she will be. Won't you, Princess?" Princess jumped in reply, whatever that was supposed to mean.

"The two of you are impossible," Noel laughed.

"Noel... are you taking Princess with you when you go back to the North Pole?"

"I don't know. I hadn't thought about it."

Kellen nodded, but didn't say anything else.

"You'll miss her if I do, won't you?"

"Yeah, but you'll miss her if you don't, and you won't have Roscoe at home anymore either."

Noel didn't say anything. She didn't know what to say. She didn't want to talk about Roscoe just then.

"I think you should take her," Kellen finally said. "That way she won't have to worry about hunting anyway. Your family is used to feeding a polar bear. You know better than anyone how to care for a polar bear, even better than Uncle Noah... We'll keep trying to teach her, but I'll feel better knowing she won't starve if she doesn't learn it."

"You wouldn't feed her if she didn't get it?"

"She's growing up. She's not a baby anymore, and I don't know anything about feeding a polar bear. It would be better for Princess if you take her."

"She'll miss you."

"I'll miss her too."

Noel thought about it for a few minutes. "Maybe we could come back to visit."

"That would be nice." Kellen sounded choked up.

The decision was far from made. Anything that was going to hurt Kellen that much was going to take more thought, but Noel let it drop for now.

Noel and Kellen spent two hours outside in the cold encouraging Princess and telling her what to do and how to do it better. She didn't have much to show for it, but that was as much of the extreme cold as Noel and Kellen were going to risk.

"Nice try, Princess. Let's go get some lunch," Noel encouraged.

Princess trotted behind them, quite proud of herself. It was still early for lunch, but Noel was starving. She hadn't had breakfast, and she had burnt a lot of extra calories. Some hot tomato soup and a grilled cheese sandwich would hit the spot perfectly.

After they ate, Noel and Kellen sat down on the bed and talked while Princess went back outside. Noel knew that Princess wouldn't go far, so she wasn't worried.

"How's training going?" Kellen asked.

"It's good. I don't beat Aunt Star every time, but I can best her now. Aunt Mary said it's because she's rusty, and I have to take on Aunt Mary next week."

"What happens when you can best her?"

"I don't know. I guess I'm finished. What more can they teach me if I can best both of them?"

"Will you leave after you've finished?"

"I have to go back to the North Pole and finally have it out with my dad."

"Why?"

"I don't want to hunt vampires."

"Then why go through all this?"

"It was my dad's idea. He made me come down here for training, said we could talk about it again when I get back. I guess he thought that the training would somehow change my mind."

"Has it?"

"No."

"If you could have any job you wanted, what would it be?" Kellen asked.

"I'd go back home to train reindeer."

"I could see that about you. You'd be great at it too."

"What about you? What would you do if you could have any job you wanted?" Noel turned the question back on him.

"Me? I'd work in the North Pole."

"Really? I thought you would say hockey."

"I love hockey. I tell everyone it's what I want, but the truth is it's my second choice."

"Why don't you tell anyone that?"

"Are you serious? Please. My dad would disown me if he knew I wanted to work in the North Pole. It's impossible anyway, so why cause problems?"

"What would you do in the North Pole?"

"I don't want you dad's job or anything like that. I don't want anything in the lime light. I want something more behind the scenes. Maybe like an assistant."

"That would be good! There's always so much to do. An assistant Santa is brilliant! You should pitch the idea to my dad!"

"I couldn't. Why would your dad want someone like me in the North Pole? How could he ever trust me after everything my dad did?"

"You're not your dad, and my dad knows that."

"Still, it-" Kellen didn't finish his sentence, because at that precise moment a growling and snorting Princess drug a seal twice her size into the cave. "She did it! Princess, you did it!"

"Ewe, why did you bring it in here? That thing is disgusting."

"Don't say that. You'll discourage her," Kellen scolded.

Kellen shoved himself away from the bed and propelled himself into the floor to congratulate Princess. He scratched behind her ears as he cooed at her. After a short wrestling match between the two, Princess tore into the seal to have a nice meal.

Noel couldn't believe how much Princess ate. It was amazing how much a young polar bear could eat. She was growing to be a grown polar bear after all, and Noel knew all too well how much a full grown polar could eat. Roscoe did love to eat!

Watching Kellen and Princess together, Noel couldn't wipe the smile off her face. He was so good with her. How could Noel separate them? Kellen wouldn't admit it, but he was lonely. He lived in a world where everyone loved the Clauses, yet he wasn't supposed to. It left his family isolated from the outside world, and he didn't have to tell her that in order for her to see it. Noel remembered the night they found him outside the dance. He looked so left out and dejected. Princess was an orphaned polar with no family left. They needed each other more than either of them knew.

"You two are a mess," Noel announced once both Kellen and Princess were covered in seal blood. Neither one seemed very concerned, so Noel went to work to magically clean up the mess.

"I better get going before my dad calls Uncle Noah to check in on me," Kellen admitted.

## Chapter Twenty-Two

Noel tried not to think any more about what she would do with Princess when she left, at least for the time being. It didn't help anything. She wracked and wracked her brain, and all it did was give her a headache. There was no way to make everyone happy.

It wasn't practical, though, for Princess to go with her. What if Dad wouldn't let go of this vampire hunting thing? If she was forced to hunt, Princess couldn't go with her. It would scare the humans to see a polar walking about like an enormous dog.

At least if Princess stayed in the South Pole with Kellen, they would both be happy. It was better for two of the three to be happy, rather than everyone being miserable. Noel just wished she could think of a way that she wouldn't be miserable either.

Monday was rough. Aunt Mary was right. Aunt Star was either rusty or had been taking it easy on her. One thing was for certain, Aunt Mary wasn't taking it easy. Aunt Mary was kicking Noel's butt. Noel had been pinned to the floor so many times she lost count.

"Time for everyone to stop and eat," Aunt Star announced. "You haven't had anything to eat all day, and that's not healthy. I'm going to have to leave in just a minute to pick up the kids, and I want to see you both eat something before I leave."

That was easier said than done. Noel was exhausted. She hurt from head to toe, and she had absolutely no appetite. Nevertheless, Noel followed Aunt Mary into the kitchen. Aunt Star had made chicken salad and tomato sandwiches. Aunt Star had been working hard to perfect her chicken salad. It had taken her a lot of trial and error, and the chicken was canned chicken. It didn't matter though. The sandwiches were delicious. Aunt Star made the best chicken salad Noel had ever tasted, which was amazing for Aunt Star, but it might not be such a good idea to mention that to Gam.

Noel somehow managed to force down the entire sandwich, and Aunt Mary dismissed her for the day.

Actually, Aunt Mary told her to go home and take a long hot bath, so Noel did just that.

Tuesday was just as rough; although, Aunt Star said Noel was looking better. Aunt Mary didn't say much. Noel had found that when Aunt Star played the sparring partner, Aunt Mary instructed, and when Aunt Mary was the sparring partner, Aunt Star instructed. Noel wondered if that was so the sparring partner could focus better, or if the other simply had a better vantage point for instructing.

By Wednesday, Noel was bruised up worse than she ever was sparring with Aunt Star. Aunt Mary's hits, kicks, and magic all packed more of a sting than Aunt Star's. At this rate, Aunt Mary was going to kill her before she ever learned anything from the sparring. Noel could barely move. The last thing she wanted to do was spend another six and a half hours sparring with Aunt Mary.

Mercifully, Aunt Mary was running late. When Noel walked in, there was no sign of Aunt Mary anywhere.

"Vivienne got called in to work, so Mary is taking the boys to school this morning," Aunt Star explained.

"She should be here soon. In the meantime, show me those bruises."

Noel was wearing loose fitting sweats over her workout clothes, so she pulled the sweats off so that more skin was revealed.

Aunt Star shook her head. "If she doesn't take it easy, she's going to do some real damage. The point is to teach you so that the vampires can't do this kind of damage, not to do it for them."

Well, that answered that question. Aunt Star had been taking it easy on her. At least now she knew the score.

"Lay down on the couch," Aunt Star told her.

Noel did as she was told, and Aunt Star started to massage Noel's bruised arms and legs. Noel could feel the magic coursing through her veins as Aunt Star worked. The tension eased, and the pain receded. Finally able to take an easy breath, Noel realized that she had not taken an easy breath in days. The torture she was putting her body through was taking its toll.

When Aunt Star stopped, Noel examined her body, and miraculously all the bruises had faded. Most of the bruises were gone. The ones that remained looked weeks old rather than days.

"Wow, thank you," Noel marveled.

"No, problem. Between Declan, with his extreme sports, and the kids, I get plenty of practice in healing bruises and scrapes."

"How much longer do we have to do this?"

"The training? Until we think you're ready to hunt on your own if that is what you so choose to do."

"But, it isn't what I choose to do."

"Regardless of what you plan to do, plans change."

"Plans maybe, but heart? I don't think I have the heart for this."

"I know, precious, but Mary didn't think she had the heart for it either."

"Yeah, and look what happened to her to change her heart!"

"Oh, Noel," Aunt Star sighed and pulled Noel into a hug. "I can't tell you the plans that God has for you. All I can do is to help you be as prepared as possible for any eventuality."

"But, what if I have a different eventuality?"

"One like what? The North Pole? I think you're prepared for that option," Aunt Star said with a wink.

"What option would that be?" Aunt Mary asked as she walked inside.

"Working at the North Pole for the rest of her life," Aunt Star ratted Noel out with a smile.

Aunt Mary sat down on Noel's other side, sandwiching her between her two aunts, and kissed her head. "I pray for that every day."

"You do?" Noel asked taken aback. "Why?"

"The life I live isn't an easy one. It's brutal. It's ugly, and it's demanding. Believe it or not, Noel, this isn't what I want for you."

"Why did you agree to train me?"

"Your dad was insistent, and I do agree with him to an extent. I believe that the Clauses can't quit on the job that God commissioned us for, but I also believe that just like Bubba was never meant to join the war, there are others who were never meant for war. I want so badly for you to be spared."

"But, you're training me... and Vivienne's boys?"

"Training the boys is different. They've got the disposition for the job, that you and I never had, and they've already got a passion for the job, that I earned through tragedy. God's plans for those boys doesn't seem to be a subtle thing. You however... I can see how badly you don't want it, and I would do almost anything to spare you."

"Then why not tell my dad, I don't have what it takes?"

"Your dad didn't ask us to train you here," Aunt Mary said with a hand over her heart. "Or even here," she continued tapping Noel lightly on the head. "He wanted you physically prepared and able. The rest is up to you."

Noel nodded. That was the gist of what Aunt Mary had told her before too. Noel stood up and said, "Well then, let's get this over with."

Thursday and Friday, Noel gave her aunts everything she had, but it wasn't enough to take down Aunt Mary. It made Noel wonder how any vampire had ever gotten past her to attack her first fiancé.

Angel came over Friday night, yet Noel didn't have the energy to do anything but sit on the bed and gossip. Too bad Noel was the topic of gossip of late.

"Everyone is talking about you and Kellen," Angel reported. "They all believe he's still seeing you. Most people think the two of you are a couple. I tried to tell my friends that wasn't the case, that you are joined by a common pet, but I didn't really think that through first, did I? That only further cemented the belief that you are involved with Kellen. You know, since the two of you have a pet together.

"There are all sorts of different scenarios on what will happen next. Some people think that you'll move down here permanently to be with Kellen despite his dad's objections. The second theory is that the two of you will run away together, somewhere neither of your families will find you ever again. Obviously, those people don't know you very well. You are a Clause through and through, and us Clauses take family very seriously. Do you know that there are even a few crackpots who think Mom and Aunt Mary are training you so that you can attack Mr. Nicola?

"Yeah, it's crazy. They say that you and Kellen fell in love back in January when the whole family was down. It was love at first sight or something like that, so the two of you planned to strong arm Kellen's dad into accepting you or staying out of y'all's business altogether. It's like an all or nothing deal. He accepts you or he loses Kellen. Like you would ever let him walk away from his family like that.

"The last rumor is that you're going to take Kellen with you back to the North Pole. It's no secret that he doesn't get along with his father most of the time. I guess they think he wants to run away. Hey, just like your mom! He's kind of like your mom's counterpart. She's the North Pole version, and Kellen is the South Pole version. Well, he would be if he ran away. That would be poetic irony. Wouldn't it? Because Kellen's dad essentially hates your mom for running away from the North Pole and seeking solace in the South Pole, and if Kellen is her counterpart, he would run away from the South Pole seeking solace in the North Pole. Do you think he'd hate his own son for that? How could you do that? How could you hate your own son? I mean that is harsh, even for Ethan Nicola"

Two things occurred to Noel in that moment. One, she was eternally grateful that Angel could carry on a whole conversation on her own. Two, the North Pole would be perfect for Kellen.

Kellen had nothing against the Clauses. He didn't always get along with his dad because of that fact. The

Clauses had nothing against him. Well... most of them had nothing against him. Shepherd was acting a little strangely lately, but he would come around. It wasn't like him to hold a grudge. The job of Santa would be impossible for anyone who did hold grudges. Kellen wanted to work in the North Pole. They needed more help in the North Pole, so why shouldn't Kellen be allowed to follow his dream?

"You do sort of have a pet together. That part is true. You would tell me if you were planning to run away with Kellen Nicola, wouldn't you?"

Noel rolled her eyes but didn't bother to answer the question. What in the world would make Angel think she was going to run away with Kellen anyway?

"Noel! Wouldn't you?"

"Yes."

"Oh, good. It's not that I don't like the idea of you and Kellen together. I don't like the idea of you running away and not telling me where you've gone. I actually think that you and Kellen would be good together. Not many people want a polar bear as a pet, but you two have that crazy thing in common. He's probably the only person on the planet that you'll ever find who loves Princess as much as you do. Then there's that running thing. I know that Mom and Aunt Mary make you do it, but I promise you come back happy every time. It's like you like running. So, is it the running you like or the running with Kellen?"

Was Angel nuts? Didn't she know that exercise released endorphins. Noel had to admit, however, that she felt a lot better after running with Kellen than she did sparing with Aunt Mary. In fact, Noel thought she might keep up the running after she got back home to the North Pole.

"There's also the way you play hockey together. It's like all you can see is each other, like the rest of the world disappears. Plus, he's really, really competitive like you, but y'all don't fight much about it. Some competitive people can't get along, because they are soooooo competitive.

"He watches you sometimes. He looks at you the way Mom and Dad look at each other. Still, you would tell me if you were dating Kellen. I tried to tell that to everyone at school, but they wouldn't believe me. I can't blame them though. If I didn't know you would tell me, I would think you were dating him too."

Noel wasn't sure how much longer Angel listed all the reasons she thought Noel and Kellen were perfect for each other. Somewhere in the middle of Angel's lengthy list, Noel drifted off to sleep.

## Chapter Twenty-Three

Noel woke up with big news and couldn't wait to tell Kellen. He was at church of course, but they didn't talk much at church. There was no sense in baiting his dad. It wasn't like Kellen was rude or anything, probably much to his dad's disappointment. Kellen smiled. He was distantly polite. He just didn't seek Noel out to chat, and she didn't him.

Bright and early, just like every weekday morning, Kellen showed up to run Monday morning. "You're up," he said with surprise.

"I am. I have to talk to you about something."

"It sounds important."

"It kind of is."

"I could come by this afternoon. We could talk."

"Don't you have homework?" Noel questioned. "Angel is busy all week long with homework, but you seem to have all the time in the world since the end of hockey season."

"I did my time. It's the end of my senior year. We're just killing time now."

"Oh."

"Come on. Let's run."

They started out at a steady trot with Princess trailing at their heels. "When does hockey season start back?"

"This was my last season. If I go pro, I'll be leaving the South Pole after graduation. If I decide to stay here, I can join a men's league. Most of the men in that league are older than me, but at least I'd have hockey if I'm stuck down here."

"You really want to get out of here, don't you?"

"I do."

"What if I told you I might have a way?"

"A way to get out of the South Pole? Please, tell me you're not suggesting I hunt vampires with you. Although, that might actually make my dad happy for a change. He hates your dad almost as much as your mom."

"Dad? What did Dad do?"

"He took your mom's side obviously. That and he sent Dad back here."

"Of course he took my mom's side."

"Exactly. Dad is stubborn."

Noel contemplated Kellen and his dad for a few moments. "You love him, though. Right?"

"Who? My dad? Yeah, I love him. I just don't agree with him."

"So, you wouldn't want to isolate him."

"Clause, what are you getting at?"

"I don't know. Maybe it isn't such a good idea."

"What's not a good idea? Does this have anything to do with your important news?"

"Yes, but now I don't know if it is a good idea. Maybe I should just forget about it."

"Forget about what?"

"You."

Before Noel could react, Kellen had come to a complete stop in front of her. Noel couldn't stop her forward momentum, so she crashed into Kellen… hard. Kellen held his ground almost causing Noel to bounce backwards to the ice. In fact, she would have too if he hadn't caught her. Kellen wrapped his arms around Noel holding her flush against his chest. The warmth radiating off him surrounded Noel and helped to fight off the harsh cold of the South Pole.

She was looking up at him when he asked, "Noel, what are you talking about? Have I done something wrong?"

"No. I just… It's not you I should forget about. It's my idea for you."

"You're idea for me?" Kellen looked confused and more than a little sick. "Maybe we should talk about this later. I'm going to school. I'll see you after school."

Kellen left then. Their run was barely half done. Whatever she had said had spooked Kellen. He hadn't trotted off. He had sprinted off as fast as his legs would carry him. He was pale, which was unusual for him, and he looked weak all of a sudden, despite the speed with which he disappeared.

What had she said, and how had he taken it?

Aunt Mary was unstoppable as usual, but at least today she appeared to be just as battered as Noel.

"I'm getting too old for training the young," she complained.

"Hey, I'm all for calling it quits whenever you say," Noel replied.

"Nice try."

"Can't blame a girl for trying."

"Yeah, yeah, I'll be ready to go again in the morning. I suggest you be ready too."

"So, are we calling it a day?"

"Yes, get some rest."

"Thank you! See you tomorrow," Noel said and rushed towards the door.

"What's the hurry?"

"I have something I wanted to do."

"This wouldn't have anything to do with a certain Nicola, would it?" Aunt Star asked with a sly grin.

"Oh yeah, I heard the two of you are getting close," Aunt Mary smirked.

"Angel told me what all people are saying, and you shouldn't believe everything you hear," Noel told her aunts.

"And, Angel told me that you spend a lot of time with Kellen," Aunt Star countered.

"We're friends," Noel shrugged. "I'll see y'all tomorrow."

Noel was antsy when she got home and decided to cook diner to distract herself. Sure, it was too early to eat, but she needed the distraction. She had just turned off the oven when Kellen called from the mouth of the cave, "Noel?"

"I'm here."

When Kellen walked inside, Noel was relieved to see he was looking better. He still looked wary, but his color was back.

"How are you feeling?" Noel asked.

"I'm fine."

"That's good. You looked like you weren't feeling well when you left this morning."

"Yeah, I'm sorry about bailing on you like that. I needed to think some things over."

"Oh."

"You cooked?" Kellen noticed.

"I did. Are you hungry?"

"I'm always hungry."

"I have meatloaf if you want some and mashed potatoes and peas."

"Thank you," Kellen said sitting down at the table to help himself.

They neither one did much talking while they ate. The whole cave was thick with tension. There was a huge elephant in the room except Noel wasn't completely sure she understood what it was. Princess left while they ate.

"Where is she going?" Kellen asked.

"To hunt. She thinks she's hot stuff now hunting on her own."

"Oh, I guess she's doing good then."

"Yep, we're pretty good teachers."

"I guess so."

After they ate, Noel moved to sit on the bed. It was more comfortable than the table chairs, and there wasn't a couch, recliner, or anywhere else really to just lounge around. Kellen cleared his throat and sat down next to Noel.

"So, you were going to tell me about your important news," Kellen reminded.

"Yes!" With all the tension in the room, Noel had forgotten all about her idea. "You want to work in the North Pole. I think you should go for it, seriously. Pitch the idea to my dad. We are always so busy. Really, we need more people to help. I think it is actually a perfect idea. I don't know why I didn't think of it before."

"That's it?" Kellen asked indignantly.

"Yes, what did you think I was going to say?"

"I thought you were going to ask me out. I've been trying all day to figure out how I feel about it."

"Gee, thanks... Just out of curiosity, what was the verdict?"

"Does it matter?"

"No, I was just curious. Why don't you want to tell me?"

"What good would it do you to know?"

"None, but it wouldn't do me any harm either. The way you're avoiding it, makes me think you have something to hide, but seriously, I wouldn't take offence. So, there's really nothing to hide. Go ahead. I can take it."

"Famous last words... There are worse things out there."

"Worse things than going out with me? Awe, that's sweet," Noel said sarcastically. Wow. Worse things out there? Worse things like what? What did that mean? Just that there were better things out there?

"So, what do you think of my idea?" Noel asked quickly trying to change the subject.

"Noel, you are so different from every girl I've ever known."

"I'm sure you meant that as a compliment, but you've got to work on your delivery," Noel sassed back. His comment had actually smarted. She was that weird Clause child. How could Angel stand it down here.

Being a Clause in the South Pole could give a girl a complex.

"Whatever, your idea is as crazy as you are. Haven't we been over this before? Why would your dad trust me to work in the North Pole?"

"Dad likes you."

"Sure, he does. Even if he does like me, there's a big difference in liking a person and trusting a person. Besides, doesn't your brother take over when your dad retires?"

"Yeah, so?"

"So, your brother hates me."

"I know he was mean. He isn't usually like that."

"Great, so it's just me who brings out the worst in him. I can't see the two of us working together."

"He's just being protective. Once he gets to know you, everything will be fine. At least think about it... Promise me."

"Fine, I'll think about it," Kellen finally agreed.

"Maybe there are worse things than working in the North Pole?"

That got Kellen laughing. Thankfully the tension in the room had dissipated. Noel much preferred relaxed Kellen to nervous and tense Kellen. Noel would like to have said that everything had gone back to normal, but it didn't. Something was different between them. It wasn't necessarily bad; it just felt different.

Chapter Twenty-Four

The rest of the week Noel was distracted by what Kellen had said. Kellen had picked up on Shepherd's odd behavior, and he thought that Dad didn't trust him. That wasn't what distracted Noel however. Kellen had thought she was going to ask him out, and he thought there were worse things than saying yes. While that wasn't a romantic proclamation that every girl wants to hear, he had actually entertained the idea of dating her no matter how slightly.

Noel wasn't sure how she felt about that. Did it change things? They were friends. Their relationship had started out strained, but they were friends now. So, what did it mean that Kellen thought they could be more than friends? Did she believe they could be more than friends?

It was like Angel had pointed out. It would cause a rift in Kellen's family. Who knew if his dad would ever forgive him? Noel certainly didn't know Ethan Nicola well enough to say. Angel didn't seem to think he would. Ripping Kellen's family apart was not an option.

"Oaf." The wind was knocked out of Noel as Aunt Mary threw her to the ground again.

"You're distracted. You've been distracted all week. You can't afford distraction when you're hunting vampires. Distraction gets you killed," Aunt Star lectured.

Aunt Mary helped Noel to her feet and asked, "What is going through your head?"

"A lot. The future, I guess," Noel answered.

"We know you have a lot to think about, and we want you to think it through and pray about it but maybe not while you're sparing."

"Could we maybe call it a day?" Noel asked not expecting much in return.

"Sure," Aunt Mary responded surprising Noel.

"Really?"

"Do you want to give her time to rethink it, or do you want to get out of here?" Aunt Star asked Noel.

"Bye," and Noel was out the door.

Angel didn't come over that night, probably because Aunt Star was hosting another dance the next day. There wasn't a special occasion. It was a just because dance. Apparently, this was normal. Noel was excited about the dance, but it wouldn't be any fun spending a Friday night alone.

Kellen showed up unexpectedly while Noel was playing with Princess trying to stave off boredom. "Where's Angel?" he asked.

"At home. Aunt Star's hosting a dance tomorrow night."

"I know about the dance believe it or not. Just because I'm not allowed to go doesn't mean I missed something that big," Kellen snapped. Yeesh, what crawled up his shorts? "Who are you going with?" he asked.

"With Angel and her family."

"No, who is your date?" Kellen was irritated. Why had he come over if he was in such a bad mood? There was no point in spreading his foul mood.

"Why would I have a date?"

"Why? Because, that's what people do. The guy takes his date to the dance."

"I didn't have a date for the last one. I went with my family."

"That was different. It was kind of a Clause family dance. This is a regular dance. For regular dances, you take a date. That's the way it works."

"I don't understand why I have to have a date. No one said anything about needing a date. I've never even been on a date."

"Really?" That proclamation brought Kellen up short. "Never?"

"Really, Kellen? I grew up in the North Pole. Who was I going to date?"

"Yeah, point taken, but what about since you've been down here. There are guys to date here."

"I haven't had time for guys."

"Well, you'd better be ready. Guys are going to be hitting on you left and right tomorrow night." And, Kellen's attitude was back.

"What is your problem? Did I do something wrong?"

"No, you didn't do anything wrong. I just don't like the idea of guys being all over you tomorrow night. They will too. Guys have been talking."

"About me? What are they saying?" Not that Noel cared what they were saying about her. At least that's what she was trying to tell herself.

"Like you don't know."

"How would I know. You're the only guy I've ever been around who wasn't family."

"You seriously don't know how hot you are?"

"Really?" Now that was a compliment. Kellen was definitely getting better at giving compliments.

"Noel..."

His words faded off, and Noel realized that he had not called her Clause all week. That was strange for him. He almost always called her Clause. Noel was still pondering this when Kellen's lips brushed against her own.

Her first kiss. It wasn't much. His lips were barely there before they were gone again, but it was her first kiss.

"Noel? Say something."

"That was my first kiss."

"Is that a good thing or a bad thing?"

Noel touched her fingers to her lips and marveled at the fact that she'd just had her first kiss.

"Noel?"

"It's a good thing, definitely a good thing."

"Good." Kellen kissed her again and again. When he pulled back, he admitted, "I've been doing some thinking. I want to pitch the idea to your father about me working in the North Pole, and I really wish you had asked me out too. Do you have to go to the dance tomorrow night?"

"I think Aunt Star would be offended if I didn't."

"I can't stand the idea of you dancing with other guys."

"It's just dancing. I've danced with my dad and brother all my life," Noel assured him.

"I want you to dance with me."

"You won't be at the dance."

Kellen shook his head like he was trying to shake something loose. Then he kissed her again. "Noel, will you be my date for the dance tomorrow night? My first dance will be your first date."

Noel didn't say anything at first. This was a mistake. It had to be a mistake. They came from two different worlds. She knew it was a mistake, but she wanted it so badly. "Yes."

Noel got up early the next day to run before going to get dressed for the dance with Angel. Angel had a bright blue dress, and Noel had a deep pink one. Noel tried several times to tell Angel about her date with Kellen, but every time something would happen. Like the time when Joy couldn't find her shoes, and Angel had to help her, or when Nickolas flooded the bathroom floor, and Angel and Noel helped Uncle Declan towel it up. There was also the time when Nickolas had made himself a peanut butter and jelly sandwich. Noel still wasn't sure if he got more on his suit or in his sandwich. Nope, all day long it had been one thing after another stopping Noel from telling Angel about her date.

Aunt Star spent most of the day at the ice rink getting it ready to house the dance. Uncle Declan acted funny, like he knew something no one else did.

When it was time to go, Uncle Declan began hem hawing around. "Just wait, girls. There's still time. Your mom is coming back here so that we can all go together."

"There's something I want to tell you while we wait," Noel tried again to tell Angel.

"Why is Mom coming here? Why doesn't she just stay there?" Angel asked her dad.

"There's a few surprises tonight."

Surprises? Did that mean that he and Aunt Star knew about her date with Kellen. She and Kellen had not really talked about how they were getting to the dance. Noel had already planned to go with Angel, so she assumed that he would meet them there. That was stupid. They should have talked about it. She should have asked. Didn't the guy usually pick the girl up for a date? Why had she not thought this through more carefully? She should have talked to Aunt Star. Aunt Star would have known what to do, or she could have called Mom. Mom didn't have much more experience with dating, but at least she would have had some advice.

Noel was going on her first date, and she knew absolutely nothing about dating. A sudden case of nerves was hitting Noel hard, and her stomach began tying itself in knots.

Out of nowhere, Mom, Dad, and Shepherd appeared. Dad and Shepherd wore tuxes, and Mom was in a lovely lavender gown.

"What are you doing here?" Noel asked.

"I missed my baby girl," Mom answered. "I asked Aunt Star if she thought it would be alright if we came down for the dance."

Noel didn't know what to say, so she said nothing. Instead, she wrapped herself around her mom in a great big bear hug. Moms had a sixth sense when it came to their children. Somehow Mom knew any time Noel needed her the most.

"Oh, did I miss the first surprise?" Aunt Star said with disappointment as she rushed into the house.

"Sorry, baby," Uncle Declan cooed and wrapped his arm around Aunt Star's waist.

"What do you mean first surprise?" Shepherd asked carefully as Noel hugged him and Dad in turn.

Aunt Star made a show of zipping her lips and throwing away the zipper.

"Do you know what's going on?" Shepherd asked Angel.

"I didn't even know you were coming," Angel complained. Angel didn't much like surprises. She liked to be in on the know.

"Well, should we go?" Dad asked.

"Finally," Joy exasperated.

"Joy Anderson," Aunt Star said in her scolding mom voice.

Joy dropped her head, but she looked more frustrated than she did repentant.

Then there was a loud knock on the door just before it busted open, splintering the wooden frame everywhere.

"I'm sorry, Mrs. Star! Coach, it was an accident! I don't know what's going on. My magic is out of control," Kellen said. He was standing in the doorway wearing a very dashing tux. He looked good in anything, but in a tux he looked amazing. Where did he get a tux at the last minute?... Aunt Star, of course. That was her second surprise.

"What are you doing here in a tux?" Nickolas asked curiously.

"I, uh," Kellen started nervously.

"Oh, the corsage! I nearly forgot," Aunt Star exclaimed.

As she took a step in Kellen's direction, Kellen stumbled back a step or two. He waved his hand inadvertently over his lapel, and a boutonniere the exact color of Noel's dress appeared on his lapel as well as a matching corsage in his hand.

"How did I do that?" Kellen asked near to hysterics.

Uncle Declan narrowed his eyes at Kellen, "How long has stuff like that been happening?"

"Since I talked to Noel last night," Kellen answered.

"And, what did the two of you talk about?"

"Lots of stuff. Mostly about tonight and the future."

"Ohhh, what about the future?" Aunt Star asked suddenly intrigued.

"Well, I-"

"Daddy, Kellen wants to work in the North Pole," Noel said taking pity on Kellen who was under the spotlight.

"Is that right?" Dad responded.

Shepherd glared at Kellen through slited eyes. "Who said we need help?"

"I did," Noel told her brother in a do not mess with me voice that she had crafted over the years dealing with a younger brother.

"Why would we need his help?"

"We do need help, and Kellen wants to help."

"What is it you want to do?" Dad asked.

"I don't want to take your job," Kellen assured. "Or yours," he added for Shepherd.

"He wants something more behind the scenes, like an assistant or a..."

"Like a partner family!" Aunt Star thrilled. "I think it's a wonderful idea the Clauses and Nicolas back together like they were always meant to be. And, don't worry about the door, Kellen. Stuff like that happens to everyone." With a dramatic flip of her wrist, Aunt Star repaired the door and rehung it on its hinges.

"But, I learned to master my magic years ago. It's never been this out of control," Kellen protested.

"Or that strong, huh? The Nikolajsen magic began to dwindle when they moved to the South Pole, because they were no longer following God's calling for them. From the moment you began to plan out a life working in the North Pole, a plan to go back to God's will, your magic started to strengthen again."

Kellen looked at Aunt Star like she might be certifiable. "So, you're saying that I'm going to be as strong as a Clause?"

"Yes and No. I'm saying you're going to be as strong as your ancestors the Nikolajsens, which is essentially as strong as a Clause."

Kellen looked at Noel, but all she could do was shrug.

"But, Mom," Joy spoke up. "I'm confused. Why did your magic not dwindle when you quit vampire hunting and moved to the South Pole?"

"That one is easy. When I came down here to marry your daddy, God had a plan for my life still. I'm here to bring the Nicolas and the Clauses back together again the way God had always intended."

"Oh."

"I think it is a great idea!" Dad burst out. "As soon as we can work it out with your dad," Dad added in a more somber tone.

"You want a job in the North Pole? Fine. Just keep your hands off my sister," Shepherd nearly growled. Then he pushed past Kellen and out the door. That last outburst was unexpected.

Chapter Twenty-Five

Well, that could have gone better, Noel thought to herself.

"Ok, everyone out the door. The dance awaits," Aunt Star pushed, and they all made the short walk to the ice rink, which wasn't housing any ice tonight.

"I'm kind of glad to have that part over with," Kellen whispered to Noel.

"Yeah, me too."

"Can I?" he asked holding up the corsage. Noel held out her arm, and he slipped it around her wrist. It was so beautiful. It matched her dress exactly, and it was her very first one ever. Best of all it matched exactly to the boutonniere that Kellen was wearing. The matching flowers were a visible sign that tied them together at least for the night. Everyone would know that they were together, and Noel couldn't think of anything sweeter.

Kellen slipped his hand in Noel's and said, "I'm glad I came tonight."

"Me too."

"Even if I can't dance? I saw you at the last dance. You're really good."

"That's because I had a good teacher. My dad loves dancing. I can teach you if you'd like."

"I'd like that very much… Clause." A grin crept across Kellen's face. Noel was glad to see it back in place where it belonged. There was nothing so beautiful as Kellen's smile.

Kellen was right about one thing. He couldn't dance. "How can someone so athletic be such a bad dancer?" Noel teased.

"This is nothing like hockey."

"Maybe Dad should teach you. He's a better teacher than I am."

Kellen tightened his hold on Noel and said, "I want you to teach me."

"What if I-"

"Mind if I cut in?" Shepherd interrupted.

"Yes," Noel answered shortly.

"Sorry, you heard the lady," Kellen said, although his tone suggested he wasn't sorry at all.

"She's my sister."

"And, tonight she's my date."

"Children behave," Noel chided. "Shepherd buzz off."

Shepherd gave a Noel a stern look. It was obvious he had more he wanted to say, but in the end, he settled for a warning aimed at Kellen, "I'm watching you."

"Enjoy the show," Kellen replied to Shepherd's retreating back.

Several songs later, Kellen was still no better at dancing. It didn't matter to Noel, though; they were having fun.

"Everyone is watching us," Noel started to notice.

"Of course they are. You're drop dead gorgeous in that dress, and I'm not supposed to be here. They're waiting to see what will happen."

"You don't think your dad will show up here and make a scene, do you?"

"Depends."

"Depends on what?"

"If any of the many people watching us decides to rat me out."

"What's Noah doing?"

"I haven't seen him. Where is he?" Kellen asked.

"Over there by the back door. He's on the phone, and he doesn't look happy."

Kellen's body went stiff when Noah started walking their direction.

"You better get out of here. Your dad is on his way," Noah warned.

"You told him I was here?" Kellen accused. He looked hurt. Noel hated seeing Kellen hurt more than she did seeing him nervous and tense.

"I would never do that to you, but Ethan isn't stupid. He figured it out on his own."

"I'm not leaving."

"You don't want to cause a scene."

"No, I don't. That's up to Dad."

"Kellen, don't do this."

"I'm tired, Uncle Noah. I can't keep pretending to be someone I'm not."

"I understand, but you don't have to do it here," Noah pushed.

"He doesn't have to come here either, but I doubt that will stop him."

Noah shook his head disappointedly but walked away. He didn't go far, yet it was a show of trusting Kellen to make his own decisions. Noel thought that said a lot whether Kellen realized it or not.

It wasn't long before Ethan walked in. Even though her back was to the door, Noel knew the second he walked through the door. All the chatter around them ceased, and there was a sudden tension that could have been cut with a knife. Noel turned to see Ethan walking quickly toward Kellen and Noel.

A scowl painted his face in an ugly light, and it was obvious that he was mad. Noah intercepted him. It looked like Noah might have been trying to talk Ethan into leaving, but of course, he didn't. Ethan Nicola was on a mission, and his laser vision was focused on Kellen and Noel.

Kellen stepped between Noel and his dad as Ethan approached them. "What do you think you're doing here? We're leaving. Now."

"No."

"Excuse me?"

"I'm staying here. With Noel. I'm going to work in the North Pole too."

Noel winced at Kellen's announcement. Did Kellen have to hit his dad with everything all at once and in front of the whole South Pole?

"Oh, no you're not. As long as you live under my roof, you'll-"

"But, that's the point. Isn't it, Dad? After graduation, I won't be under your roof anymore."

Ethan fixed Noel with a stare. She could see Dad over Ethan's shoulder. His entire body was tense. His hands were fisted at his sides, and Mom was holding him back.

"She'll hurt you in the end," Ethan warned Kellen. "She's just like her mother."

"No, Dad, she won't. She's not her mom, and Wynter Clause isn't the one who hurt you. You did that to yourself. She wanted to stay friends. She reached out to you numerous times, but you were too stubborn. You're the one who caused all the pain. You're the only one still holding onto that mess. Look dad."

Snow began to drift lightly to the floor all around the three of them.

"Cut that out," Ethan said to Noel.

"She's not doing it, Dad. I am."

"How? What?"

"It was the first thing I was able to do last night after telling Noel I was going to ask her dad for a job in the North Pole. I was lying in bed. I was hot and thinking about the snow falling outside. Then the next thing I knew, it was snowing in my bedroom. I'm not asking you to like it, just to accept me for who I am. I love Noel Clause, and I'm moving to the North Pole."

Love? Did love always work this quickly? Noel wasn't sure what to think or even what to feel. Was that where their friendship had been leading to this whole time? Kellen Nicola just told his dad and everyone else that he loved her. Did she love him?

"What you're going to do is get home so that we can talk about this," Ethan barked.

"I'll be home by curfew."

"You'll get yourself home now."

"Ethan?" Noah said quietly.

"Don't," Ethan said in a deadly tone. "You did this. You and Wynter turned my only son against me, and if that wasn't enough, now she's trying to take him away from me."

"That's not true," Noah said patiently. "No one wants to take Kellen away from you."

An older couple approached, a couple that Noel couldn't remember having ever met.

"Ethan, you're causing a scene. Go home," the lady said.

"You called Mom and Dad," Ethan accused Noah.

"He didn't have to. We've been here all along."

"And, no one here is missing the scene you're causing. Go home," the man said.

"You're taking her side?" Ethan asked, his voice cracking.

"We're not choosing sides, son. Just go home," the lady told him.

Ethan let out a defeated sigh and turned to leave. Before he turned, Noel could have sworn she'd seen a tear roll down his face. Mom always said that he was hurting more than he hated. Maybe she was right after all.

"Kellen," the woman addressed, "I know this isn't what you want to hear, but your dad told you to go home. It's time for you to go."

Kellen made a disgusted grunt that reminded Noel of his father. Then he kissed her quickly and rushed out the door.

The older lady put a hand to Noel's face. "You look like your father so much. I always did adore that boy."

"Thank you, Mrs. Vikki," Mom said from behind the woman.

Mrs. Vikki turned around and pulled Mom into a hug. "Oh, how I've missed you Wynter Clause. You don't visit us down here nearly enough."

"I'll try to keep that in mind."

Visit? Noel didn't remember ever seeing this woman once in her life before tonight.

Next Mrs. Vikki looked to Dad and charged, "I'll expect you to take good care of my grandson when he's in the North Pole with you. He's the only one I have, you know."

"I'll do my best."

"I dare say you'll have your hands full. He's a handful, that one, but he's a good kid."

The man shook Dad's hand and kissed Mom's head before striking up a conversation about the Christmas Eve operation with Dad. Noel missed what was said, because Angel pulled her away.

"Oh my goodness! That was intense," Angel sighed. "And, you just kissed Kellen Nicola. You've got to be like the most popular girl in the South Pole right now."

"You know what? I don't care what anyone else thinks of me," Noel replied, but it wasn't entirely true.

She might not have cared what most of them thought of her, but she cared very much what Kellen thought of her. He said he loved her, and she was pretty sure that she was falling in love with him too. Family was important to her, so like it or not, she cared what Kellen's parents thought of her.

## Chapter Twenty-Six

Noel woke up the next morning with a heavy heart. Her parents and Shepherd went back to the North Pole last night, without her. Of course, her training wasn't done yet, but that didn't matter much in the grand scheme of things.

By lunch, Noel had decided she wanted to confront Kellen's parents. It probably wasn't any of her business. No, it definitely wasn't any of her business, but she couldn't help but feel guilt and a little glimmer of hope that she could help.

Then again, she should probably just stay out of it. She had no right to get in the middle of family business.

Something was up with Aunt Star and Aunt Mary too. They were huddled together whispering, even though it was only the three of them at the house. When their powwow came to a finish, Aunt Mary quietly slipped out the door.

"Where is she going?" Noel asked.

"We're going to call it a day early. You've been making good progress," Aunt Star answered.

"That's laughable. I haven't managed to pin Aunt Mary once."

"No, you haven't, but you've been holding your own lately. She's not been able to pin you nearly as easily as she did at first. That's a big deal. Mary does this every single day of her life in a do or die situation. She can't afford to let anyone best her, so the fact that you are holding your own is quite impressive… Speaking of impressive, that was a pretty monumental announcement Kellen made last night."

"Yeah, but I think it will be good. Dad and Shepherd could use the help, and Papa could finally fully retire the way he wants to."

"Yes, that would be good, but I was remembering when Kellen told his dad he loved you."

Noel sighed heavily. "Aunt Star, how did you do it?"

"How did I do what?"

"How did you win over the South Pole? Everyone loves you. How did you make them like you?"

"First off, you can't make someone like you. Secondly, it took time, Noel, and a lot of it."

"I don't want Kellen to choose me over his family, but I don't want him to not choose me either. I don't know what I want. I can't be the reason that he loses that bond with his parents. Why can't they just like me? Did Uncle Declan's parents like you?"

"Oh, heavens no. They were like most of the South Polers and resented all Clauses, but I only made it worse when I mentioned Anthony."

"Dad? How did mentioning Dad make it worse?"

"Declan's mom was, is, very fond of your dad. It broke her heart to hear me talk about him being in the North Pole with Wynter."

"How did you get past it?"

"I left."

"But, you and Uncle Declan got married," Noel protested.

"Thanks to North."

"What did Uncle North have to do with it?"

"Well, as you can imagine I was more than a little upset when I left. I was devastated, and it hurt North to see me like that. He came down here to give Declan a piece of his mind; except, when he found Declan, Declan insisted that North take him to me. In the end, it was Declan who settled it. He told them that if they made him choose, he'd choose me, so we found a compromise we could all live with."

"That's what I'm scared of though. What if Kellen gives his dad the same ultimatum? There is a lot of hate in that man. What if he chooses to lose Kellen?"

"Hate and hurt are both very strong emotions, and sometimes it is impossibly difficult to see the difference. Love and time are the only way to overcome hurt."

"You think I should give Kellen's dad time?"

"What do you think you should do?" Aunt Star returned.

"I'm not sure anymore. Part of me wants to go and talk with his parents, but what if I only make it worse?"

"Or, what if you go over there with your heart full of love and build a foundation? You can't build a house strong enough to last without a strong foundation."

"What if I don't have love in my heart?"

"Do you love Kellen?"

"I think I do?"

"What you need to remember is that these are Kellen's parents. Whether you like the way they went about it, they are responsible for raising the young man you love, and that is something about them that you can love and appreciate."

"Yeah, you're right. I can do that. It might not work."

"There's always that possibility, but what have you lost."

"Self-dignity."

"When I left Declan, I went straight to the North Pole, where I fell completely apart. I cried constantly. I stopped getting out of bed, and I just gave up on life. There was nothing dignifying about it. Sometimes the hard road is the most dignifying route to take. If you give up before you've tried, isn't that as good as giving up your self-dignity?"

"I guess you're right, and I have somewhere I have to go. Thank you, Aunt Star."

Noel went straight to Kellen's house. At least she thought it was Kellen's house. She had never actually been there. She knocked nervously on the door and waited anxiously for an answer. Looking down at her clothes, Noel wished she had made a stop by the cave to get cleaned up first. She was still dressed in workout clothes and smelled like she had been working out.

Noel asked herself what she was doing there. She didn't even know if they were home. Kellen was still in school. She could wait until he got out and come back then. The door opened, and it was too late to turn back now.

A woman opened the door. She was cute for lack of a better description. Her chubby cheeks, big round eyes, and naturally rosy lips gave her a look of innocence. "Can I help you?" she asked.

"Are you Kellen's mom?" Noel inquired.

"Yes, and you are?"

"What are you doing here?" Ethan barked from behind Kellen's mom.

Well at least Noel had the right house. "I wanted to talk to you for a minute if that's alright."

"No, it's not alright. You have some nerve coming here after what you pulled Saturday night. Get out of here."

"Ethan, just shut up! For twenty years I've been nothing but loyal to you and your opinions, but I want to meet the young lady who our son has fallen in love with. Come in," she invited.

Noel moved slowly and carefully as if she were approaching a tiger. Mrs. Nicola led her through the foyer to the living room and motioned for her to sit down on the couch. Ethan plunked down into a recliner and crossed his arms across his chest. He was staring at the floor with a scowl on his face. He was making it abundantly clear that he was closed off to anything Noel had to say.

"Your name is Noel? I think that's what I've heard Noah say," Mrs. Nicola started.

"Yes ma'am."

"Tell me about yourself."

"There's not much to tell. I have one younger brother and grew up mostly isolated in the North Pole."

"What are you doing here in the South Pole?"

"My aunts are training me to hunt vampires… but I don't want to be a vampire hunter," Noel didn't know why she added that last little tidbit. She was over sharing.

"Are your parents making you?"

"Well, my dad is sort of. He said we could readdress it when I got back home after training, but he feels really strongly about it."

"Wasn't he a vampire?" Mrs. Nicola clearly knew the answer already.

"Yes, which is exactly why I don't want to do it. Mostly that, and I don't think I have what it takes to do it."

"What about your mom?"

"I don't know exactly how she feels. They're trying to show a united front. You know how parents do it."

"I do know how parents do it," Mrs. Nicola laughed.

"I don't think she strictly agrees, but I definitely don't. I want to stay in the North Pole where I can work with the reindeer. They're getting older, you know. If no one is working with the fawns there won't be any young reindeer to take the place of the older ones who are beginning to slow down. This will already be Cupid's last year to make the trip. I have two good fawns who are ready to come up, but they're young. They need discipline and steadiness in their routine training. I've been gone so long now that it will take some serious work to get them back on track. No one else works with the reindeer the way I do. Mama doesn't have time. Dad has a strong bond with the sleigh team, but he hardly knows the fawns. Gam and Shepherd don't have a knack with animals, and Papa wants to fully retire so badly he can taste it. Technically he retired when I was just a baby, but no Santa can retire fully. Not really. The job is just too much for one man to undertake. The whole family has to help out."

"It sounds like you enjoy working with animals. You have that in common with Noah."

"Yeah, Noah's great. He taught us to make bottles for our orphaned polar bear. I call her Princess."

"Our?"

"Yes, um, she's kind of mine and Kellen's. "We've both worked a lot with her. Kellen fed her while I was gone, and we both taught her how to hunt."

"You and Kellen? You taught a polar bear to hunt?"

"Yes, ma'am. She was just a little baby when we found her next to her mother. Her mother was dead. She's still young but getting big so fast."

"You talk like she's a pet or something."

"She is. We had a pet polar bear at home. His name was Roscoe. We'd had him my whole life, but he recently died."

"I'm sorry to hear that." Mrs. Nicola looked like she might have been more baffled than sorry.

"I took it pretty hard. That was when Kellen went with me to the North Pole."

Ethan grunted and shifted in his chair.

"Kellen got in some pretty big trouble. I'm really sorry. I wasn't trying to get him in trouble. I just wasn't thinking."

"It's understandable," Mrs. Nicola sympathized.

Ethan made a disgruntled noise and shifted again. Noel watched him apprehensively for a moment or two before turning back to Mrs. Nicola. "Kellen is really great. He's one of the kindest people I know. He held my hand and tried to comfort me the day we lost Roscoe. He was kind to me when I gave him no reason to be. When I found out who he was, I was so sure that he would hate me at once simply because of my last name, that he would hold onto some old grudge that had nothing to do with me. He didn't. He was cordial. It took me a while to realize I was the one holding a grudge." Noel looked timidly at Ethan. "I knew how much you hated my mom, and I held that against Kellen. Once I let go, I realized what a good guy he was."

"How did you meet Kellen?" Mrs. Nicola asked.

"Um, maybe I shouldn't say. I don't want to get anyone in trouble."

"You won't get anyone in trouble," Mrs. Nicola assured her, but it was obvious that Ethan didn't offer the same assurances.

Noel shrugged but didn't tell.

"Tell me this. Do you feel the same way about Kellen as he does about you?"

"I think so," Noel admitted.

"You think?"

"Yes, it was sort of a slow thing. No, slow isn't the word for it, because I was surprised it could happen so quickly. I didn't see it coming though. It kind of snuck up on me. We were friends, good friends mind you, but just friends. Then out of nowhere we were more."

"I see," Mrs. Nicola said, yet she didn't look like she saw anything. She was staring in Noel's direction but focused somewhere off in space. "Do you know who you remind me of? You remind me of the mystery girl Ethan used to talk about constantly."

Ethan growled and stood up. Mrs. Nicola glanced at him briefly then returned to her distant stare. "Oh, I was so jealous of her back then."

"You never told me that," Ethan revealed softly. Everything about him softened all at once. His stance was less tense. His scowl fell from his face. The hate and frustration in his eyes disappeared, replaced by love and tenderness. He had been keeping a close eye on Noel, but now he had eyes only for his wife.

"I was scared I'd lose you," Mrs. Nicola admitted to Ethan.

"That would never happen."

"I know that now, but back then our love was so new and so young. When we found out she was a Clause, I was too embarrassed to admit I was ever jealous of her, and it always upsets you so much to talk about her. After relations with the North Pole began to ease, it just seemed silly to bring it up."

Ethan pulled his wife into his arms and snuggled her close. This must have been the side of Ethan Nicola that Mom always talked about with adoration.

"Mom, is there anything to eat?" Kellen's voice boomed through the house.

Was it that late already? School was out? Kellen's parents didn't budge, and he stopped short coming upon the scene in the living room.

"What's going on?"

# Chapter Twenty-Seven

With long strides Kellen moved quickly to Noel's side. Laying his hand on the side of Noel's face he whispered softly, "Did he hurt you?"

Ethan snorted but otherwise ignored the insult.

"Yeah right. Your dad might not like me very much, but he's hardly dangerous."

"Are you sure you understand why my dad went to the North Pole? I told you the story of what he did."

"No one got hurt."

"Not seriously, sure, but Uncle Noah says that was because he was outnumbered."

"He doesn't seem so bad to me. You don't seem to be suffering at his hand."

"What? No, Dad would never hurt me."

"He loves you. He only wants to protect you."

"I know he loves me, but-"

Before Kellen could finish what he had been about to say, Ethan interrupted, "I had a knife to her throat. If my hand had so much as slipped, I could have killed her."

"Oh, Ethan, you never told me that part!" Mrs. Nicola gasped.

Noel just bet he didn't. Mom had a scar across her throat that she never talked about. Figured it came from Ethan. "She still has the scar."

To Ethan's credit, he grimaced.

"Ethan Nicola, you put an actual knife to someone's throat?" Mrs. Nicola scolded.

Ethan winced and dropped his head to his wife's shoulder. "I was in a bad place. I wish I could undo what I did, but I can't."

"You should tell my mother that. Even if you don't like her, I'm sure it would make her feel better just to know you don't want to kill her. She doesn't talk about you, you know, except when she asks Noah if you are well."

"I can't take back what I did."

"Are you in a better place now?" Kellen challenged as he moved to put himself more fully between Noel and his Dad.

"You don't remember that long ago, do you?" Mrs. Nicola asked.

Kellen didn't answer.

"Your dad was like a different person during that time. He was someone I didn't recognize. He was so driven by revenge that I worried we'd never get him back."

"Did we ever get him back?" Kellen had the good sense to wince at the pain that flashed across his dad's face.

This was getting ugly. Noel hadn't meant to make things worse. "I should go."

"I'll come with you," Kellen responded.

"No. I mean, you should stay and talk to your dad."

"I want to go with you."

"You need your family."

"I like this girl," Mrs. Nicola said. "I agree with her. Kellen, you and your father are overdue for a heart to heart. Noel, we are having dinner at Ethan's parents' house tonight. I'm sure they would love it if you could join us."

Noel looked to Kellen for a clue what she should do or say. His small imperceptible nod of his head had her answering, "Ok."

It was normal to be nervous when having dinner with your boyfriend's family, but it was nearly sickening to be having dinner with your boyfriend's family when they didn't like you. Ok, Kellen's mom might like Noel, but that didn't mean that Ethan ever would.

Noel walked up to the door. This was the right house… she hoped. She knocked efficiently on the door and waited. She didn't wait long before Kellen answered the door with a wary expression.

"You don't have to do this if you don't want to," he told her.

Noel swallowed over the lump in her throat and took a deep breath. Then with more confidence than she felt she said, "I want to do this."

"Ok, don't say I didn't warn you."

Kellen took Noel's hand and lead her into the living room where his mom and dad sat across from a man who must have been Kellen's grandfather. Noel recognized as the man from the dance even though they had not been introduced.

For as much as Kellen looked like his dad, Noah looked like his. Kellen's grandfather had the same dark hair and blue eyes sitting atop chubby cheeks that Noel was used to seeing on Noah.

"Mom," Ethan called out without getting up.

An older lady came running into the room asking, "Is she here? Is that her?" The lady walked right up to Noel without ever slowing up. "You must be her. I didn't get a good look at you at the dance last week. You look just like Anthony! Honestly, I can't see Wynter in you at all!"

"Granny!" Kellen exasperated.

"Oh, hush. It's true, and I didn't hurt her feelings at all. Did I, sweetheart?"

"No ma'am."

"See there. Now, you have to tell me everything. Start with your name."

"Noel."

"Noel Clause. And, you have a brother too. Right?"

"Yes, ma'am. His name is Shepherd."

"Bear with me. I haven't talked to your mom since the night she left all those years ago. I get all my updates from Star."

Ethan grumbled under his breath making it obvious that he didn't appreciate his mother's association with Aunt Star or her interest in Mom.

"Alright, Noel, I'm Mrs. Vikki, and this is Mr. Norm," she said pointing at the older gentleman in the room. "Everything is ready. We're just waiting on Noah and Lorelei. He got held up at work. You two sit down and get me updated on your family."

Kellen pulled Noel across the room to the couch where his parents were sitting.  He sat down next to his dad leaving just enough room on the end for Noel to sit. As soon as she sat down Kellen threw his arm over her shoulders.

"How are your parents doing?" Mrs. Vikki asked.

Noel launched into a full list of what her family had been up to lately and a description of their family dynamics. As she spoke, Kellen started running his hands absently through her hair. She wished he wouldn't do that. It was only a matter of time before his fingers got tangled in her mass of curls. At the moment he was, no doubt, teasing it into a frizzy mass. Curly hair was finicky that way.

"Well, this is interesting," Noel recognized Noah's voice. She turned around to see him frozen in the entryway.

"Noah, nice of you to join us. I'm starved. Let's eat," Mr. Norm said.

Everyone stood and followed Mr. Norm into the kitchen.

"How was work, Uncle Noah? Did you know that Noel works with animals too?" Kellen greeted.

"I did know that actually," Noah replied.

"Noel, you didn't tell me that," Mrs. Vikki said, "and Noah, shame on you for not keeping us up dated."

"I didn't know you wanted to know, Mom."

"Of course, I want to know!" Then she looked back to Noel properly ashamed, of what Noel had no idea. "I guess you want an explanation."

"Oh, you don't owe me anything. It's ok, really."

"No, I know, but I want you to know how sorry I am. Do you have a basic idea of what happened with your mom when she was living down here?"

"Yes, ma'am."

"I didn't know what to do when Wynter was outed as a Clause. I was mad, disappointed more like, that I had been deceived by the girl who I had come to think of as my own, my only girl. After that night she was gone, and everyone hated her on principle. I followed their lead just to keep down confrontation. I do hate confrontation. I guess I'm a coward that way. The day that Noah came home with that forced treaty, it was such a relief that I could breathe again."

"I felt better too. It was almost like we had been justified for not wanting to give up on Wynter," Mr. Norm added.

"Not justified, Norm. We didn't stand up for her like we should have. We weren't justified, but we had been given permission to love who we loved. I do love your mother. You'll send her my apologies, won't you?"

"I will. I'm sure she'll be overjoyed."

"Do you think? It's not too late? She let me hug her the other night, but she could have been trying to be polite and not cause a scene."

"Never, not with Mom. She still loves all of you too. I can tell."

"Maybe we could all get together some time. New Year's would be after the big Christmas rush. Ask her. Ask her if she'd like to come for New Year's."

"I'll do that."

Mrs. Vikki's eyes were glistening with unshed tears. Noel focused on her plate. The food was delicious. "This is very good," Noel said using her fork to point to her food.

"Thank you."

"I hear you are making post-graduation plans," Mr. Norm said to Kellen.

"We've not discussed it yet, Dad," Ethan interjected.

"It doesn't matter. As far as I'm concerned it is a done deal," Kellen returned.

"Well, I want to hear about it. What about you, Jackie," Mrs. Vikki asked Kellen's mom.

"Oh, I do too. Lorelei?"

"I definitely want to hear about these plans," Lorelei agreed.

"I'm going to the North Pole. Nothing is worked out yet, but Noel's dad thinks it's a good idea," Kellen filled in.

"I do too," Mrs. Vikki enthused. "What would you be doing?"

"Mom, don't you think that's a little far from home," Ethan protested.

"The last I heard, Kellen was leaning towards professional hockey. Professional hockey would take him far from home too. At least in the North Pole he'll be around people who can get him back home for a visit in an instant... I assume you can all do that transporting thing Star does?" Mrs. Vikki added to Noel.

"Yes, Granny, Noel can do it, but I may not need her help for much longer," Kellen piped up.

"That's what I want to hear more about," Mrs. Jackie, Kellen's mom said.

"Me too," Lorelei seconded.

"What is it we're talking about?" Mr. Norm asked.

"Kellen's magic has been growing exponentially the last few days," Noah answered.

"Is that right? How so?"

"Well, the first time I noticed it was when I made it snow inside. Since then I've been doing all sorts of things that I've never done before, things I shouldn't be able to do. Mrs. Star thinks that my magic is getting stronger because I decided to go to the North Pole."

"Why would she think that?" Mrs. Vikki asked.

"Haven't you read the journals?" Noah asked his mother.

"No, I want to so badly, but they're always checked out, and there's a long waiting list."

"You're direct descendants of the Nikolajsens. I bet Aunt Star would make a copy for you," Noel predicted.

"Oh, that would be wonderful! We could put it with the family records. I'll have to make a point to ask Star."

The rest of the meal was lovely. Ethan was quiet but polite, which was more than Noel had ever expected from him. Everyone else talked, and Noel felt like she had always been a part of the family.

Mom would be so excited to hear that Mrs. Vikki wanted her to come for New Year's. Noel couldn't wait to tell her. What she couldn't decide was whether to go that night to the North Pole or wait and call home the next morning. The decision was made for her, however, when she noticed the time. It was late when they left Mrs. Vikki and Mr. Norm's house, and everyone back home would have been long since in bed.

"I'll walk you home," Kellen offered.

"It's a school night," Ethan gestured.

"It's not like we're doing anything this close to graduation."

"Come on, Ethan Nicola. You can walk me home," Mrs. Jackie said pressing against Ethan's side.

Ethan's face softened as he placed a kiss on the top of Mrs. Jackie's head. "Fine, but don't dilly dally," he told Kellen without turning his attention from his wife. They started walking in the opposite direction from Kellen and Noel.

Princess met them out front of the cave. She was jumping about in an excited fashion. Kellen bent over to ruffle her fur and cooed, "There's my girl."

The errant thought hit Noel how tall Princess was getting. It wouldn't be long now before Kellen didn't have to lean over at all.

"Kellen? Princess has never known how to live in the wild, not really."

"Yeah, I thought that was the point of us teaching her to hunt."

"Yes, but it is a far cry from knowing how to hunt to surviving in the wild with other animals."

"I guess so. What's your point?" Kellen asked.

"My future is still so uncertain. If I don't make it back to the North Pole to stay, you'll take her with you when you go?"

"Of course I will, but you'll go with us."

"How do you know that?"

"Because, we'll be together no matter where we go," Kellen said, and he kissed her. Noel knew that she would never tire of Kellen's kisses.

He hadn't been in her life for very long, but now Noel couldn't imagine her life without him. She didn't want to imagine a life without Kellen Nicola.

## Chapter Twenty-Eight

Noel was beginning to make headway against Aunt Mary the next morning when there was a knock on the front door.

"Keep going," Aunt Star chimed as she moved out of the room.

Aunt Mary swept Noel's feet out from under her in a move that Noel did not see coming. "What did Star tell you about distractions?" Aunt Mary griped.

"I'm trying. You should try kicking your butt sometime. It isn't easy."

"Alright then." That was Mrs. Vikki's voice.

Noel looked up from the spot where she was pinned to the floor. There was Mrs. Vikki towering over her looking startled. "Hi, Mrs. Vikki."

"Hi, Noel... What on earth are you doing?"

"We're training."

"What kind of training?"

"Vampire hunting, but I'm afraid Noel has a long way to go," Aunt Mary answered.

"Don't be so harsh, Mary. She had made great progress," Aunt Star defended. "She's learning much faster than we did, faster than anyone I can remember. We started training from a much earlier age, and you know it."

"Great progress won't keep her alive, and you know that."

"She's got us there, Noel," Aunt Star agreed with her sister as Aunt Mary helped Noel to her feet.

"Why would you want to train for vampire hunting?" Mrs. Vikki asked.

"It's a Clause tradition."

"What can I do for you, Vikki?" Aunt Star asked in a bubbly voice.

"Oh, I wanted to talk to you about the Nikolajsen journals."

"What about them?"

"I've not had the chance to read them yet, but I was wondering, do you think we might get a copy to put with our family records?"

"Oh, that is a wonderful idea! Your family is the direct descendants of Christopher Nikolajsen. I don't know why I didn't think of it before!"

"To be honest, I would never have thought to ask if it hadn't been for Noel. It was her idea," Mrs. Vikki admitted.

"Good job, Noel!"

Noel blushed under her aunt's compliment. "You know, Mrs. Vikki hasn't been able to read the journals because of the waiting list. The South Pole could really use more than one copy."

"I could do that," Aunt Star said contemplatively. "Multiple copies would be unnecessary and take up space in the long run, but a few temporary copies would be useful, I imagine."

"Oh, Mrs. Vikki, I talked to Mom this morning. She's thrilled, just like I said she would be. She said she'd love to come," Noel recalled.

Mrs. Vikki nearly teared up then. "Good, that makes me so happy. Tell her to be sure to bring the family with her."

"I will."

Aunt Mary was paying close attention to the conversation, so Noel took that opportunity to attack. In no time, Aunt Mary was pinned to the floor underneath Noel.

"Distractions, Aunt Mary, distractions," Noel smiled.

"You little stinker," Aunt Mary laughed.

Much to Noel's surprise, the day ended in a second, this time real, pinning of Aunt Mary. Noel didn't hold her pinned long before she leaped to her feet to break into a happy dance. Aunt Mary sat on the floor with an appreciative smile, and Aunt Star doubled over laughing at Noel's impromptu dance.

Noel relived the moment that afternoon when Kellen got out of school. They sat in the cave with Princess while Noel described how she took down Aunt Mary with vivid detail.

"So, does that mean you're done with your training?" Kellen asked once Noel's story was done.

"I didn't even think to ask. I was just so thrilled to have finally done it."

"Oh well. You'll tell me before you leave to go back home, won't you?"

"Of course I will… How much longer do you have in school?"

"Three weeks."

"Maybe we can go together."

"What if your dad isn't ready for me that soon?"

"He will be."

"Noel," Kellen said, clearly a warning.

"If he's not, you can help me with the reindeer until he's ready."

"Deal."

As it turned out that afternoon had been a turning point in Noel's training. She didn't always pin Aunt Mary after that. She didn't even pin her fifty percent of the time, but she could pin her from time to time.

What really threw Noel for a loop was when Aunt Mary and Aunt Star both came at her at one time. It wasn't a tag team deal. They actually attacked simultaneously. It took some doing and a whole lot of practice, yet somehow Noel managed to hold her own. She couldn't beat them or even one of them, but they couldn't beat her either. When they all three went to throwing magic around in quick, repetitive succession, the house very nearly vibrated with all the pent up magic.

"Defeating multiple attackers is hard even for seasoned veterans," Aunt Star confided. "The important part is that you can stay alive long enough to escape."

As far as Aunt Mary and Aunt Star were concerned, Noel had completed training. At least it was as much effort as they were willing to spend training someone who had no intention of ever hunting vampires. And, Noel had no intentions. She had prayed and prayed, yet she still felt no pull towards vampire hunting. The more time that passed, the more determined she became to stay in the North Pole.

Plans were being made for Kellen to move to the North Pole. He would officially make the move two weeks after graduation, and as Kellen made plans with Dad, Noel made plans with Kellen about their future. They weren't rushing into anything immediately following graduation, but there was time. Kellen thought that two years to settle into his new job and new life in the North Pole sounded reasonable. Noel, on the other hand, was already plotting out in her mind where they would build their house and how many kids they would one day have, and that was the only argument she needed against vampire hunting.

As long as Kellen was in the North Pole, so would Noel.

Epilouge

Noel sat in the stands waiting to catch a glimpse of
Kellen. He wasn't inside the auditorium yet, though.
All the graduates would march in together. The whole
process was foreign to Noel. There was no need for
so much pomp and circumstance when you were
homeschooled. It was exciting though.

Everyone was there, Kellen's family of course.
Aunt Star had come with her family. Angel was sitting
next to Noel, and both girls were bouncing around in
their seats like they were going to jump out of their
skin. Aunt Mary had come with her family. Kris was
obviously bored, but he hadn't wined anymore since
Uncle Blaine had whispered who knows what
into his ear.

Mom and Dad were there. Noah was sitting to Dad's left and Mom to his right. Ironically, Mom had managed to wedge herself between Dad and Ethan. Ethan seemed to be taking it well enough. He wasn't very chatty, but at least he was tolerant. To be honest, Noel was more worried about Mrs. Jackie who was sitting on her husband's other side. She was stiff and kept glancing across Ethan to see Mom.

Mrs. Vikki and Mom had an emotional reunion. It was equal parts wonderful and emotional. It was everything they had wanted to say and do the night of the dance but held back due to the public arena. Noel no longer thought that the two women were going to make it until New Years without seeing each other again. They had already been talking about how Kellen would need to keep in touch after moving to the North Pole and that Mom could maybe accompany him. They also talked about Mrs. Vikki and Mr. Norm coming up to the North Pole.

Mom told Ethan and Mrs. Jackie that they were welcome to visit Kellen at the North Pole any time they wanted. Mrs. Jackie and Dad went stiff at that invitation. Maybe the world wasn't ready yet for Ethan Nicola's return to the North Pole, but maybe someday.

At last the music started and the graduates began to walk inside the auditorium and take their own seats.

"Look, there he is! There he is!" Angel said as she pointed with one hand and punched Noel's side frantically with the other.

Noel leaned forward to get a better look. Kellen turned to make eye contact and winked at Noel. Noel couldn't wipe the silly school girl smile off her face. Kellen sure did make those funny black robes look good. Then again, Noel was beginning to realize that she was a little biased.

The whole ceremony took longer than Noel would have expected. She was pretty sure most of the speakers liked to hear themselves talk just for the sake of talking. Eventually they made it to the part where each of the graduates' names were called. Kellen walked across shook a man's hand and accepted his diploma.

It was almost over, thank heavens. Kellen had said he had a surprise for everyone after graduation, and Noel couldn't wait.

As soon as the ceremony was over, Kellen and his parents invited Noel, her parents and her brother to their house. Mrs. Vikki and Mr. Norm beat them to the house, where Mrs. Vikki and Mrs. Jackie had

everything ready to go. There was food in the crockpot and a wide array of desserts.

Mom and Ethan mysteriously disappeared once they started eating. Dad didn't look worried, so Noel tried not to worry either. Shepherd was quiet, but he was acting strangely even for him. It didn't matter. He'd have plenty of time to get to know Kellen. Noel was sure that Kellen would win him over with enough time. At least for now he was being civil.

"You don't think my dad has killed your mom and is trying right now to hide the body, do you?" Kellen whispered into Noel's ear.

Noel could feel his smile against her ear and knew he was teasing. "Your dad has been shockingly hospitable, and I think he almost likes me even."

"You're hard not to love," he said and kissed her neck.

"What's the big surprise?" Noel asked self-consciously changing the subject.

"You'll see."

"So mysterious."

Kellen just smiled.

Mom and Ethan chose that moment to walk back in. "Let's eat," Mrs. Jackie announced as soon as she saw them reappear.

"Everything alright," Dad asked Mom lightly.

"I think so," Mom answered emotionally, and Noel could have sworn she saw Mom's eyes tear up for just a second.

The food was delicious. Not that Noel had expected anything different; since she and Kellen had been dating she had learned that both his mom and grandmother were great cooks.

"Who's ready for cake?" Mrs. Jackie asked.

"I am!" Mom said with a little bounce. That was weird. Noel had never seen Mom get that excited over cake before. Mom liked sweets but not that ecstatically.

"Kellen, sweetheart, are you ready for cake?" Mrs. Jackie asked.

"I'm more than ready," Kellen answered.

All across the room everyone pulled out their phones as if ready to take photos or videos. What was Noel missing? Mrs. Jackie hadn't said anything about making a special cake for Kellen's graduation. It could have slipped her mind. She had been busy lately. It wasn't worth worrying over. Everyone else had their phones out, so she could have someone send her the picture.

Mrs. Jackie came back in carrying a big sheet cake. It was iced in white, but that was all Noel could tell from her sitting position. Then Mrs. Jackie did the strangest thing yet. She placed the cake directly in front of Noel.

Noel looked down and noticed the beautiful lettering on the cake that read: Will you marry me?

Noel knew Mrs. Jackie wasn't purposing, so she turned her attention to Kellen, only to find him in the floor on one knee holding up the most beautiful engagement ring Noel had ever seen.

*Wrong Turn Fairy Tales*

Gwynn worked hard to live up to her family's expectations putting away all childish things and even a few childhood friends. Now she is about to marry Addison, a very sensible, very rich businessman, but before she can say yes to his proposal, she finds herself falling through one fairy tale after another. Will she find her happily ever after with her very own prince charming, or has her fairy tale taken a wrong turn?

Exclusively found from Barnes & Nobles for Nook Book.

*More Than Instinct*

Kat had a past best left forgotten. Jackson had a past he couldn't get over, but when circumstances throw them together in a dangerous game, they had to find a way to work together. What they would find was that, "This whole mess had bonded them in a way that could never be undone."

Available from your favorite bookstore.

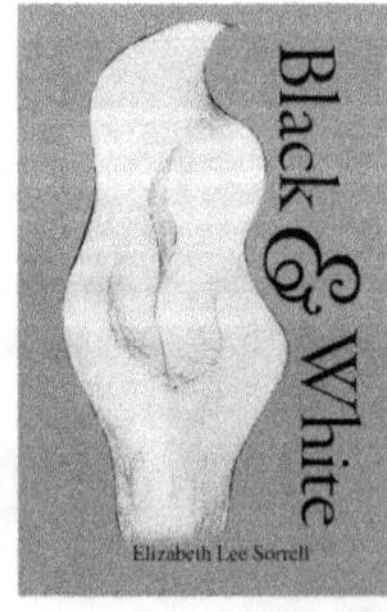

*Black & White*

Shantelle White has been with a top secret branch of the CIA from its very beginning. Jayson Black is one of the branches top operatives. When funds get tight Shantelle and Jayson are forced together to find a solution. Will they find out where the money has gone and who is behind it before all their agents are gone?

Available from your favorite bookstore.

*Red and the Big, Bad... Wolf?*

Zeke had a secret to keep and a duty to fulfill. Romance was not a part of his plans, but fate had different plans. Roxie was a busy and successful business woman. After a random mugging, Roxie found herself caught up in a much larger and deadlier crime wave. Now she'll have to count on her brother's friend, Zeke, to get her out of trouble.

Available from your favorite bookstore in paperback and ebook.

*Home Runs, Double Plays, & Spies*

Lindsey Sanders, working for a small-town newspaper, just landed the job opportunity of a lifetime reporting on the Atlanta Braves. There was only one small problem. Brandon Cobb was a spokesman for the FBI who Lindsey had spent a significant amount of time interviewing over the years. It was no secret that they couldn't stand one another. When Brandon walked onto the field under the name Kevin Baxter, would Lindsey keep his secret, and if so, how long could that last?

Available from your favorite bookstore in paperback and ebook.

Don't forget to check out the Children's Books
from Elizabeth Lee Sorrell

# About the Author

Elizabeth Lee Sorrell is an Alabama native. As gifted teacher with her Bachelor's in Early Childhood Education and Elementary Education, and her Master's in Early Childhood Education, she teaches in the Federal Head Start program.

When not teaching, or leading in the Nursery as the Nursery Coordinator of her church, she is with her family and dear friends, probably reading or writing a book. She loves to spend time with her nieces. Elizabeth is a Christian. She cheers for the Auburn Tigers, and the Atlanta Braves. As a big baseball fan, she has, more than once, written stories in the world of MLB, and watches as many games as she is able.

She enjoys pairing up with Sandra JS Coleman for her covers, layouts, and illustrations. Sandra, Elizabeth's sister, is a graphic designer and an illustrator.

Learn more at www.ElizabethLeeSorrell.com

Elizabeth Lee Sorrell is an Alabama native. As gifted teacher with her Bachelor's in Early Childhood Education and Elementary Education, and her Master's in Early Childhood Education, she teaches in the Federal Head Start program.

When not teaching, or leading in the Nursery as the Nursery Coordinator of her church, she is with her family and dear friends, probably reading or writing a book. She loves to spend time with her nieces. Elizabeth is a Christian. She cheers for the Auburn Tigers, and the Atlanta Braves. As a big baseball fan, she has, more than once, written stories in the world of MLB, and watches as many games as she is able.

She enjoys pairing up with Sandra JS Coleman for her covers, layouts, and illustrations. Sandra, Elizabeth's sister, is a graphic designer and an illustrator.

Learn more at www.ElizabethLeeSorrell.com

# Colophon

Cover Design, Cover Photography, and interior
layout designed by Sandra JS Coleman using
Adobe CC software.

The typefaces used on the cover and interior are
Azo Sans Uber, Marydale, Origins, and Mrs Eaves OT.

Azo Sans Uber was designed by Rui Abreu. He is a
Portuguese type and graphic designer, working on
commercial fonts since 2006. Marydale was designed
by Bryan Willson in 1993. It was his first font designed
based on a friend's handwriting. Origins was designed
by Laura Worthington, a typeface designer from
Washington State. From the mid '90s until 2010 she
trained and worked as a graphic designer. With a lifelong
fascination in lettering and typography, she turned it
into a business, publishing her first typeface in 2010.
Laura's faces are primarily based on her own hand-
lettering and calligraphy. Mrs Eaves was designed by
Zuzana Licko in 1996. Licko emigrated to the US in
1968 and graduated from Berkeley in 1984.

The book was printed in the United States of America,
on 50lb white paper, perfect bound, with a gloss cover.